EAKY
NALONE

PER CREEPY CAMP

To future me. Your glasses are on your head, and
the car keys are in the fridge ~ Barry Hutchison

For James George, I hope you enjoy this book
as much as you love your favourite spoon
~ Katie Abey

STRIPES PUBLISHING
An imprint of the Little Tiger Group
1 The Coda Centre, 189 Munster Road,
London SW6 6AW

A paperback original
First published in Great Britain in 2017

ISBN: 978-1-84715-812-3

BEAKY MALONE

SUPER CREEPY CAMP

BARRY HUTCHISON

ILLUSTRATED BY KATIE ABEY

CHAPTER 1

THE DRAW

"So," said my best mate, Theo, hiking up the steps beside me, "I've been thinking."

"Congratulations," I said, stepping aside to let a group of more enthusiastic pupils pass us on the way to class. "Did it hurt?"

"Hilarious," said Theo. "But listen, you know how you can only tell the truth now?"

"I had noticed," I said. I'd been unable to tell a lie since a weird woman called Madame Shirley stuck me in an even weirder truth-telling machine in the back of her shop a few weeks ago.

"Well, I've thought of all the things you've told me over the years that I reckon might not be true."

"All the things?" I said doubtfully.

"Well, OK, not all of them, but some of them," said Theo. We rounded a corner on to the science floor, then headed up the next set of stairs. "And I think this is the perfect time to find out if they're actually true."

"I'll save you the bother," I said. "They probably aren't."

"Number one," said Theo, ignoring me. "Do you really have monkey DNA?"

"No."

"Are your parents spies?"

"Which one?" I asked.

"Either," said Theo.

"No."

6

"Did you really break your nose training for the Olympics?"

"Yes!"

Theo stopped. "What? No way!"

"Yeah. I decided I was going to be an Olympic gymnast and tried to do a backflip," I said. "It didn't end well."

We carried on up the stairs. "I mean, if you're asking was I hand-picked by Team GB to represent the country at the Olympic Games like I told you I'd been? No. Did I knee myself in the face while attempting acrobatics in my living room? Yes. Yes, I did."

"Smooth," said Theo. "I'd have loved to have been there to see that."

"Yeah," I said. "You could have called the ambulance."

We arrived on the English corridor and stepped up the pace. We had spent months perfecting our technique for getting between classes, figuring out the exact speed we could walk so we arrived late enough to miss a little bit of each lesson but not late enough to get into trouble.

"What do you think Doddsy has got in store for us today, then?" Theo said.

I puffed out my cheeks and shrugged. "An English lesson, probably," I said.

"Yeah, that sounds about right," said Theo, then his eyes widened. "Wait! No! It's today, isn't it?"

"Yes," I confirmed. "Of course it's today. Technically, I suppose, it's always today..."

"No, I mean today's the day!" Theo said. "Today's the day they draw the names for the Wagstaffe Cup!"

The Wagstaffe Cup – or, to give it its full, completely idiotic title, the Winston and Watson Wagstaffe Cup of Competitive Chummery – was a cup awarded to the winner of an inter-school contest between our school and nearby Foxley Hill School. Every year, a Year Seven class was chosen – this year it was ours – then five pupils were randomly selected to take part. Today was the day the draw for the team was being made.

"I wouldn't worry about it," I said. "It's a pretty big class. What are the chances of us being picked?"

"Tiny," Theo agreed. He smiled. "Let's go find out who's unlucky enough to make the team."

Wayne Lawson was looking at me. This was *not* good. Wayne looking at you is never positive news,

especially if he's looking at you the way he was looking at me – eyes narrowed, nostrils flared, mouth curved into a nasty-looking smirk. It had only been a couple of weeks since I'd been partnered with Wayne on the school trip to Learning Land, after the

teachers had somehow got it into their heads that I was bullying him and that spending time together would help us become friends. In fact, Wayne was the one bullying me and over the next few hours I'd only narrowly avoided being pummelled into a lumpy paste by his massive fists.

Luckily I'd managed to expose him as the two-faced sneaky bully he is, while also showing everyone on the trip video footage of him being frightened almost to the point of crying by a man dressed as a clown. To say he was looking for an opportunity to get his own back was a bit of an understatement.

Unbelievably, Wayne had managed to avoid getting into trouble by giving his dad – who happened to be our head teacher – some sob story about feeling like he wasn't getting enough parental attention. He'd told him that his behaviour at Learning Land had been a cry for help, which probably sent his dad into panic mode.

Mr Lawson already had one son in prison and the last thing he would've wanted was for Wayne to end up there, too. Although, to be fair, it's probably where he belongs.

So, ever since Learning Land, all the teachers had been sucking up to Wayne even more than usual and basically letting him get away with murder.

Not *literally*, of course, although I wouldn't put it past him.

This meant Wayne was getting all kinds of special treatment – like right now, when he was being allowed to draw out the names of the pupils taking part in the Wagstaffe Cup. Mrs Dodds had wanted to be the one to do the draw but Mr Lawson had told her not to be so selfish.

While Mrs Dodds sat behind her desk, trying not to look annoyed, Mr Lawson took a small rectangle of paper from Wayne's hand and unfolded it. A flicker of irritation flitted across his face as he read the name aloud.

"Dylan Malone."

I glanced around the class, looking for the poor, unfortunate soul who'd just had his name drawn. It was only when I saw everyone staring at me that the words filtered through into my brain.

"Wait. That's me," I said. "I'm Dylan Malone."

A ripple of laughter passed around the class.

Mr Lawson tutted his annoyance. "Well, that doesn't exactly bode well for the contest, does it?" he said. "If our first team member isn't even sure of his own name."

"It's just that everyone usually calls me 'Beaky', sir," I pointed out.

"Yes, well…"

"Because of my massive nose."

"Yes, thank you, Beaky," said Mr Lawson. He shook his head and quickly corrected himself. "*Dylan*. Thank you, Dylan. I think we get the picture."

Another rumble of laughter went around the class. Mr Lawson twisted his face into the boggle-eyed stare he does when he's trying to look scary. He calls it the "hawk-eye" but it makes him look more like a constipated pigeon, if anything.

"Right, that's enough!" he yelled. "I'm sure I don't need to remind you just how important the Wagstaffe Cup is to the school. It is not a laughing matter. What is it not?"

"A laughing matter," mumbled the class in unison.

It might not have been a laughing matter but when it came to the annual contest with Foxley Hill School, our school was pretty much a laughing *stock*. Apparently no one had told Mr Lawson that, though.

The contest had originally been set up by the heads of our school and Foxley Hill, who were identical – and highly competitive – twin brothers. They were also, by all accounts, completely mad.

The original rule book for the Winston and Watson Wagstaffe Cup of Competitive Chummery was eight-hundred pages long, written in Latin and – if rumours were to be believed – bound in guinea-pig fur. The list of rules included one about pupils not being allowed to have more than two legs each and six pages dedicated to acceptable sock colours for competitors.

Over the years, most of the rules had been chucked out and the ones that were left were only a bit mad, rather than stark raving bonkers.

"For thirty years, a team of our Year Seven pupils has competed against a team from Foxley Hill School," said the head grandly. "Once a year, over two days, we have matched wits, knowledge, strength, skill, speed and stamina, determined to be crowned victor!"

Theo raised his hand. "And have we, sir?"

"Have we what?"

"Ever been crowned victor?"

Theo knew full well what the answer to that question was. Everyone did.

"Well, no, not as such," admitted Mr Lawson. He rallied quickly. "Still, I have a good feeling about this year!"

His eyes fell on me and he seemed to deflate a little. "Or I did have," he muttered.

"I shouldn't be on the team, sir," I said.

Mr Lawson raised an eyebrow. "Oh? Why not."

"Because I don't want to be," I said, completely

truthfully. Completely truthfully was the only way I could say anything these days. I hadn't been able to tell a single lie since exiting the truth-telling machine and believe me when I say it wasn't for want of trying.

Mr Lawson looked almost hopeful. "And you don't want to be on the team *because*...?"

"It'll be rubbish and we'll probably lose," I said. "And because you have to spend the night in the woods and I'm scared there might be bears."

The head teacher shook his head. He looked almost as disappointed as I felt. "Not a good enough excuse, I'm afraid. Unfortunate as it is, I'll have to keep you in." He turned to his son. "Wayne, next name, please."

Wayne rummaged in an upturned hat and pulled out another neatly folded piece of paper. Mr Lawson took it and unfolded it.

"Evie Green."

Across the room, Evie Green blinked in surprise. Most of the time, no one really noticed Evie because they were too busy looking at her glamorous best friend, Chloe, instead. Evie glanced over at me and half-smiled.

"Cool," she said.

"OMG, I'm so glad it's you and not me," said Chloe. "Seriously, you have no idea how relieved I am right now. If I had to take part in that stupid  contest, I'd die. I swear. I'd *literally* die."

"Chloe Donovan," said Mr Lawson, taking the next name and reading it.

Chloe immediately flopped forwards, her head landing on her desk with a *thonk*. For a moment, I thought she had actually died but then she let out a groan of frustration and sat up again. "Fine.

Whatever. I'll do the stupid contest, as long as I don't have to do anything."

"You'll have to do things," sighed Mr Lawson, and Chloe's head *thumped* on to the desk again.

"Right, two more to go, let's get a move on," said the head, his dream of winning the cup for the first time fading rapidly.

Wayne rummaged in the hat and pulled out two more slips of paper. "Theo," said Mr Lawson, barely bothering to look up.

"YES!" I cried, leaping out of my chair and throwing my hands into the air. The rest of the class, including Theo, stared at me. I cleared my throat. "I'm happy about this news," I announced, then I sat down again.

Mr Lawson unfolded the last piece of paper. "And… Wayne!" he said, sounding pleased for the first time since my name had been pulled out.

"NO!" I cried, leaping out of my chair and throwing my hands in the air again. "This is *terrible*!"

"Nonsense!" said Mr Lawson. "Wayne is one of the best athletes in the school. He's the fastest runner in the year."

"Yeah, because he's always chasing after people to beat them up," I said. "Or, more recently, running in terror from clowns."

Wayne began to snarl at me, then immediately covered his hand with his mouth and put on a surprised look when his dad turned round. "I can't believe I'm going to be on the team for the Wagstaffe Cup!" he said with a grin. "We won't let you down, Dad!"

Mr Lawson tried his best to look cheerful. "Well... You know, I think we might have a chance this year," he said. "What do you think, Mrs Dodds?"

Behind her desk, Mrs Dodds gave a sullen shrug. "Yeah, suppose."

"Yes," said Mr Lawson, properly brightening now. "With Wayne's physical prowess – not to mention his talent for spelling – Evie's general knowledge and everyone else's... Um..." He reached desperately for something positive to say about the rest of the group but fell short. "*Other skills*, I really do think we've got a very good chance of winning."

"Wow," said Theo, leaning across to me. "And some people still think *you're* the biggest liar in school."

"Don't you think it's weird?" said Theo between mouthfuls of chicken baguette. It was lunchtime and we were wandering the school corridors, trying to avoid talking to anyone.

It was the safest place to be, since I'd lost my ability to lie. Talking to people usually resulted in something bad happening, as I found it impossible to keep the truth in. If someone had a personal hygiene issue, for example, like B.O. or bad breath, I'd tell them. Loudly. Even if they were a teacher.

Especially if they were a teacher.

I'd humiliated myself more times than I could remember and humiliated Theo almost as many. He knew all about the truth-telling machine and, unlike everyone else I'd tried to tell, actually believed me.

I'd stopped going to the canteen the day after the trip to Learning Land, when I'd accidentally proposed to Miss Gavistock the dinner lady in front of half the school. On bended knee and everything.

Luckily Theo had rugby-tackled me to the floor then told everyone he'd dared me to do it for a laugh. I don't know what I'd do without him, which is why I was so glad he was on the team for the Wagstaffe Cup.

"Don't I think *what's* weird?" I asked.

"The team."

"Well, Wayne's weird, yeah. And terrifying. Mostly terrifying, actually."

Theo shook his head. "No, I mean … look who's on it. There's you. Wayne is desperate to get you when there are no teachers around."

"Thanks for reminding me."

"So he can kick your head in," Theo continued.

"Yes! I know. No need to go on about it."

"Then there's Chloe, who you reckon Wayne fancies."

I nodded. "I don't reckon, I know."

22

"There's no way Chloe would agree to take part without Evie, and — oh, what's this? — she's on the team, too. What a coincidence."

"So you're saying Wayne fixed it? He deliberately rigged the team so we'd all be on it?" I said. "Why would he pick you, though?"

Theo shrugged. "Probably for the quiz round. I'm pretty clever."

I burst out laughing. "No, it won't be that."

"Hey! I know some stuff!" Theo protested.

"You have a weird and, if I might say so, tragic knowledge of buses."

"Coaches," Theo corrected.

"Same thing," I said.

"It's not the same thing," Theo insisted.

"*And*," I continued, ignoring him, "you know more video-game cheat codes than anyone," I said. "So, unless they've introduced an Xbox Coach Driver simulator quiz, I doubt that's why he picked you."

Before we could discuss it any further, we turned a corner and there, dead ahead, was my sister, Jodie. She and a few of her friends were striding along the corridor towards us and Jodie didn't look happy to see me at all. About five different expressions flitted across her face in the space of two seconds. They ranged from "unbridled rage" to "absolute terror" with a quick detour to "panicked confusion" somewhere along the way.

PANICKED CONFUSION

UNBRIDLED RAGE

ABSOLUTE TERROR

"Quick, quick, the gobstopper!" Theo said.

Frantically I rummaged in my pocket and took out a clingfilm-wrapped giant gobstopper. Jodie's friends all clucked and chattered as the group swept towards us but Jodie just stared at me, her face turning red as it twitched and contorted through its range of emotions.

Unwrapping the enormous candy ball, I shoved it into my mouth just as Jodie's little tribe passed.

"Hey, Beaky!" said one of Jodie's friends.

"Hrmff-ung," I said, the gobstopper making it impossible to reply.

Jodie looked relieved and even gave me a faint nod of acknowledgement as she passed, then – panic over – went back to chatting with her friends.

As soon as they had gone, I spat the gobstopper back into the clingfilm and wrapped it up again.

"Phew!" I breathed. "That was close."

Of all the people I'd embarrassed with my truth-telling, Jodie had come off worst. I'd turned some of her friends into mortal enemies, got her into trouble with Mr Lawson, and told several boys that she not only fancied them, but had made a horrifying sort of collage drawing of them, picking out her favourite bits of each and combining them into some weird Frankenstein's monster.

That last one, in particular, hadn't gone down well.

The gobstopper had been her idea. Whenever I saw her in school, I was under strict instructions to shove it in my mouth so I couldn't speak. At first, I'd refused but when she'd promised to shove her fist in my mouth instead, I'd reluctantly given in.

It worked, for the most part, although I did spend almost a full minute one day performing an elaborate mime in an attempt to let her friends know about a recent bout of diarrhoea she'd had.

 Luckily my miming skills leave a lot to be desired and they'd thought I was pretending to be a frightened chicken.

"What were we saying again?" I asked, falling into step beside Theo once more.

"Just that I'm the best chance our team has of winning the cup," said Theo, finishing his baguette.

"Ha! You're an even worse liar than I am," I laughed, then I shrugged. "It might be all right, though, I suppose. The contest, I mean."

"Unless Wayne murders you in the woods."

"Yeah, unless that happens, obviously. That'd put a bit of a downer on it," I admitted. "Assuming he doesn't, though, it might be OK. It might even be fun!"

"Yeah." Theo shrugged. "It might be."

"But it probably won't be, will it?"

"No, it'll probably be terrible," said Theo.

And he was right.

CHAPTER 2
MUM'S BIG ANNOUNCEMENT

"Quick, quick, in you come," said Dad, standing at the front door and beckoning me and Jodie inside. "I want to show you something!"

Jodie and I both groaned at the same time. Dad works from home writing (terrible) advertising jingles for the radio and whenever he's excited to show us something, it usually means he's got bored of being by himself all day and has done something ridiculous.

28

Like the time he'd used four thousand matchsticks to build one really giant matchstick, or the time he painted the entire living room in glow-in-the-dark paint, thinking it'd save electricity.

Our front door opens straight on to the living room, and Jodie and I stepped through, bracing ourselves for whatever fresh madness Dad had wasted his day on. I looked around cautiously. The walls weren't illuminated in green so that was a good start. There were no matchstick constructions, no ill-advised science experiments and Dad hadn't painted his face to look like a tiger. Maybe he hadn't been messing around all day, after all.

"I've taught Destructo how to dance!" Dad announced.

No, he definitely had been.

Jodie and I both blinked at the same time.

"You've what?" asked Jodie.

"Look!" Dad grinned and pointed over to the couch. Destructo, our Great Dane, stood on it. He was wearing a frilly pink tutu and I'm sure he actually blushed when Jodie and I saw him.

"I know what you're thinking," said Dad.

"That you've lost your mind?" I said.

"Ha ha! No!" said Dad, although even he didn't sound all that convinced. "You're thinking, 'I can't wait to see this!'"

"We're definitely not thinking that," said Jodie.

"I'm thinking, 'Should I call the RSPCA?'" I said.

Dad picked up his guitar and went to stand

beside Destructo. "Just you wait. This is going to make us famous."

He launched into a fast strum and began to sing. "Dance dog, dance dog, *dance* dog, dance dog, dance, dance, dance dog, dance dog…"

Destructo looked from us to Dad and back again.

"Dance dog, dance dog, dance, d-dance, dance…"

Destructo turned so his back end was pointing in Dad's direction then noisily broke wind.

Dad recoiled and stopped strumming. "Ugh, wow," he grimaced, pulling his T-shirt up over his nose. "That's disgusting."

"I don't think that technically qualifies as dancing," I pointed out.

"No," Dad admitted.

"I mean, he just farted in your face, really."

"Yes, I noticed." Dad sighed. "I don't understand

– he was dancing around all over the place earlier."

"Was he, though?" asked Jodie, dumping her bag in the corner. "Or did you fall asleep on the couch and dream it?"

"Like that time you thought there was an octopus in the kitchen," I said. "And kept screaming hysterically when we opened the door."

"No!" said Dad. He shifted uncomfortably. "I mean … I don't *think* it was a dream." His eyes went to Destructo. "Although … he did seem *very* agile."

"If it was a dream, how come he's wearing a tutu?" I asked.

"Ha! Exactly," said Dad triumphantly. "That proves it!"

"It proves you've put our dog in a massive frilly dress, that's all," said Jodie, easing the tutu over Destructo's back legs. "Where did you get a tutu this size, anyway?"

"Trust me," said Dad. "You don't want to know."

Jodie sighed. "No, probably not. Hopefully one day – years from now – he'll get his dignity back."

"I'm going to the toilet for a massive poo," I announced.

Dad frowned. "Bit too much information there."

"Sorry, it just came out," I said. "A bit like the massive—"

"Yes! We get it!" said Jodie, cutting me off before I could finish the sentence. "Just go."

"And don't sit there for ages playing games on your phone like you usually do!" Dad called after me. "Mum's bringing a takeaway home, and if you're not back down, I'll eat yours!"

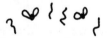

One successful toilet trip later (104 minutes – a Jodie-annoying personal best), we all sat round the table, tipping different-coloured curries out of little plastic tubs and on to our plates.

"So, what's this in aid of?" I asked. "You never get us takeaways."

"We had fish and chips that weekend Jas and Steve were here," Mum pointed out.

I glanced across at Jodie. How could I forget? Mum had sent me and Jodie on a quest to find  a chip shop, and it was during this fateful search that we'd stumbled upon *Madame Shirley's Marvellous Emporium of Peculiarities*, the place where I'd lost all my lying skills. The shop – and Madame Shirley – had disappeared almost immediately after we left and I'd been trying to find them both ever since.

"Yeah, I wish we hadn't had those," I said. "You know, what with the weird shop and the truth-telling machine and everything."

"Oh, good, *this* again," Mum muttered. She didn't believe us about the truth-telling machine, and thought it was some strange joke I was playing, even though Jodie had backed me up on all of it.

Mum picked up a naan bread. "I didn't fancy cooking tonight." She glanced over at Dad. "You see, we've got a bit of an announcement."

"You're getting divorced," I guessed. I leaned back in my chair. "Well, I can't say I'm surprised. I'm amazed you've lasted this long, actually."

"No! We're not getting divorced!" said Dad. He shot Mum a worried look. "We're not, are we?"

"No, dear," said Mum, patting his hand. She took a deep breath. "I'm running for head of the PTA!"

"The PTA?" I said.

"That's right!"

"Is that the ethical treatment of animals by people?" I asked. "Because, if so, Dad had Destructo wearing a tutu earlier."

"That's PETA," Jodie tutted. "She means the Parent Teacher Association."

"Oh," I said.

Mum frowned. "*Oh?* That's all you have to say? 'Oh.'"

I thought for a moment. "Um … yep. Yep, that's pretty much it."

"This is huge, Dylan!" said Dad, but I could tell his enthusiasm was mostly put on for Mum's benefit. "Being the head of the PTA is a big responsibility."

"Massive," agreed Mum.

I wrinkled my nose. "Yeah, but does anyone really care? Or even know what it is?"

"Yes!" said Mum and Dad at the same time.

"I've been on that PTA since Jodie started at Nutley Grange," said Mum, stabbing a chunk of chicken with her fork. "I've given that school some of the best years of my life and it's time my contributions were recognized properly." She shoved the meat in her mouth and chewed. "Of course, I'll have to beat that Green woman."

"What, She-Hulk?"

Mum tutted. "No! Not a 'green woman', *Helen* Green. She's standing, too. And she's got a good chance. She's *very organized*," Mum said, whispering the last two words for some reason, as if they were a big secret.

"Aha!" said Dad, reaching for his guitar again. "But does she have a campaign song?"

"You haven't," said Mum.

"You haven't," said Jodie.

Dad began to strum. "Oh, he has," I groaned.

"She's amazing," Dad sang. **"She's tremendous. Whenever there's a meeting she'll be there. Claire Malone. Claire Maloooooone. CLAIRE MALOOOOONE!"**

He finished with a few dramatic chords, then stood up and took a bow. "I thank you."

37

"You do realize that's the theme tune to *Danger Mouse*?" I said.

Dad shook his head. "What? No, it isn't."

"It is," said Jodie. "I recognized it right away, and I've never even seen *Danger Mouse*."

"It isn't. Listen," said Dad. He began to strum again. **"She's amazing. She's..."** He stopped playing. "No, you're right. It's the theme to *Danger Mouse*."

"Thanks anyway, dear," said Mum, patting him on the hand. "The rest of the PTA will be voting on the new head at the next meeting, so we have to hit the campaign trail now, and hit it hard!"

"*We*?" Jodie and I both said at the same time.

"I expect there'll be some press interest over the next few days," said Mum, ignoring us both. "That's why I got my hair done."

All eyes went slowly to Mum's head. "I knew that!" Dad yelped. "I mean… I spotted that right away but was waiting for just the right time to mention it. It's beautiful."

"Really nice, Mum," Jodie agreed.

"It looks the same," I pointed out.

The temperature in the room dropped a full degree. "No, it doesn't," said Mum. "It's completely different."

"Of course it's different!" Dad laughed.

"Yeah, you can hardly recognize her," Jodie chipped in.

"OK," I said. "How is it different, then, Dad?"

Dad's mouth dropped open. He shot daggers at me for several long seconds but I just smiled back. Eventually, he turned and glanced at Mum's head. "Well, it's … different in a lot of ways."

"Such as…?"

"Well, I mean, obviously it's … a different length?" he said, then he saw a flicker of something on Mum's face. "I mean the same length. Mostly the same length, but the colour is…"

"The same," said Mum.

"Yep. And quite right, too. It's a lovely colour, why would you want to change that?" said Dad. He banged his fist on the table, as if the answer had suddenly come to him. "It's curlier!"

"Straighter," Mum sighed.

"*Was* curlier. Before, I mean," said Dad, recovering pretty well. "Now it's definitely straighter. Definitely. Any idiot could see that."

Dad quickly shoved three massive forkfuls of rice in his mouth so he didn't have to speak any more.

"How much did it cost, Mum?" I asked, watching Dad closely to see his reaction.

"I got a great deal, actually,"

Mum said. "It was only fifty."

Dad coughed so violently he sprayed rice all over the table and floor. There was a sudden movement from behind me as Destructo began hoovering up the rice that had landed on the carpet. With his mouth, I mean, not the vacuum cleaner. He's a bright dog but not that bright.

"Fifty?" Dad spluttered. "What, *pounds*?"

"No, pence, dear," said Mum. "Of course pounds! I've got to look my best for the press."

"I doubt they're going to be interested," I said.

"Nonsense! The head of the PTA is an important figure in the community," said Mum. "After all, the PTA is instrumental in the running of the school."

"Do you pick the teachers?" I asked.

"Well, no," said Mum. "But we do get to look at them."

"*Look* at them?" said Jodie.

"Sounds a bit creepy," I said.

"No, I mean, we get to look over their applications."

"And give input to the head on their suitability for the job," said Dad, backing Mum up.

"Well, no, not *input*, exactly," said Mum.

"Not *input*, that's not what I meant," said Dad, still doing his best to be supportive. "But you discuss their suitability at your meetings, don't you, dear?"

"Well, no, we can't do that," said Mum. "Data protection and everything. The school could get into pretty serious trouble if we did that."

"Right," said Dad. "I see."

He shoved another three forkfuls of rice in his mouth.

A thought suddenly occurred to me. "Wait … could the PTA get me out of the Wagstaffe Cup?"

Mum and Dad's faces both lit up. "You've been picked for the Wagstaffe Cup?" asked Mum.

"Ha ha! Hard luck." Jodie snorted.

"Way to go, Dylan!" added Dad, through his mouthful of rice. "It's a big honour being asked to represent the school."

"Yeah, not really," I said. "We think Wayne cheated and pulled my name out of the hat so he can beat me to a pulp in the woods when no one's looking."

"Wayne? Lawson?" snorted Mum. "He wouldn't hurt a fly."

I threw up my hands in despair. "Seriously, how *does* he do it?"

Jodie's phone bleeped. "No phones at the dinner table," said Mum. "I thought we'd all agreed."

"Well, you and Dad agreed," I said. "Jodie and I both voted against it, so technically it's a tie."

Jodie reached into her pocket. "I better check. It might be an emergency."

"An emergency?" said Dad. "Did you join the fire brigade and not tell us?"

Jodie swiped her screen. She stared at it for a few seconds, her eyes widening in horror. "Beaky, my room. Now!" she hissed.

"Hang on. You haven't eaten your dinner!" Mum pointed out.

Muttering under her breath, Jodie scooped up a massive pile of curry on to a piece of naan bread, then spent the next several seconds shoving the whole lot into her mouth.

"Are you going for a world record?" Dad

asked, as we all watched her struggling with the overloaded naan.

Once the Korma-laden bread was finally all stuffed in, she turned to me again.

"Mmm rrrm, Bmmky," she mumbled through the mouthful. "*Nnnw!*"

Then, before I could protest, she grabbed me by the nose, yanked me out of my seat, and marched me through to her bedroom.

CHAPTER 3

BEAKY'S BLOG

Jodie flopped on to her bed, opened her laptop and began typing in the address bar. I knew within the first few letters what was about to happen.

"Look, I can explain," I said.

Jodie forced down her curry-soaked naan. "Can you, Beaky? Can you really?"

She finished typing then hit return. The browser window changed to show a website with a yellow background and two words in a large, blue font at the top.

"Beaky's Blog," Jodie read. She scrolled down.

"You're probably thinking that's mine," I said.

Jodie shot me a glare, then scrolled down and continued to read. "A complete and detailed account of everything that's happened to me lately, Dylan 'Beaky' Malone."

"I mean, it *is* mine, obviously," I said. "But I had a very good reason for doing it."

"And what might that be?" Jodie demanded.

I smiled weakly. "I wanted to."

"Let's see what you've written, shall we?" Jodie snapped, clicking the link marked "Entries".

"No, don't!" I protested, but it was too late.

There, in 16 point Arial Bold typeface, were the words: "My Sister Has a Moustache."

"Oh my God, it's true," Jodie gasped. "This is what Sasha just texted me about."

Jodie's lips moved silently as she read the blog entry. Her scowl deepened with every line.

Slowly I backed towards the door but my truth-telling got the better of me. "Sneaking away. I'm sneaking away," I announced.

"*Stay right where you are!*" Jodie yelled, in the voice she usually reserves for telling Destructo to stop eating the telly.

She finished reading the blog post and glowered at me. "You told everyone I use cream to burn off my moustache!" she yelped. "That's not true."

"Yes, it is," I said. "It's that little pot you keep behind the shampoo in the bathroom cupboard."

Jodie blushed. She scrolled down the list of posts. "What else have you got on here?" she demanded.

I bit my lip but the truth was determined to come out. "Loads! Stuff from your diary, a write-up about all the boys you fancy, a live blog of that time you spent forty-six minutes lip-synching and dancing in front of your mirror, pretending you were on *The X Factor*..."

"WHAT?!" Jodie roared. She leaped up from the bed and pushed me against the wall. "It says it's a detailed account of *your* life, not mine. Why's it all about me?"

"It started off about me and just sort of snowballed," I admitted. "But there *is* embarrassing stuff about me, too. About Miss Gavistock and about wetting myself in Madame Shirley's Machine." I bounced excitedly, which isn't easy when you're being pressed against a wall. "Oh! Oh! And some other people have been in touch about Madame Shirley! They've read the blog and emailed me to say they'd seen her."

"What people?" Jodie growled, her fist drawn back.

"I don't know, I haven't had a chance to reply to them yet. People. Other people. They've seen Madame Shirley's shop."

"Wait … so random people are reading the blog?" said Jodie, her voice dropping into a low growl. "How are they finding it?"

I knew I couldn't lie my way out of this but I could try to be economical with the truth. "*Someone* may have submitted the link to several thousand search engine and website directories."

"It was you, wasn't it?"

"Yes," I said. So much for being economical.

"How many people have seen it?"

I swallowed. "Well, I haven't checked the stats in a couple of days…"

"How. Many."

"Just about eighty thousand or so."

Jodie's jaw dropped. "Eighty thousand?!"

"Last week, yeah. This week will probably be higher. That moustache post is really drawing the crowds."

Jodie stepped back, shaking her head. She looked like she was about to go into shock. "Why would you do this to me?"

"It was supposed to help. I thought if I wrote all this stuff down, it'd stop me saying it out loud and embarrassing everyone," I said.

Jodie pointed at her laptop. "You told eighty-thousand people I use hair cream to remove my moustache!"

I shifted uncomfortably. "Yeah, in hindsight it was probably a mistake," I admitted. "Oh, and I expect it'll be closer to two hundred thousand by now. Like I say, it's a *very* popular post."

"Delete it," Jodie barked. "The whole thing. Delete it right now!"

"I can't."

Jodie's face darkened. "What do you mean, you can't?"

"Because it might lead us to Madame Shirley," I said. "And because I knew you'd tell me to delete it one day, so it asks for a two-hundred-character randomly generated password when you try to remove any posts. It can't be tampered with. Not even by me."

Jodie stared at me in horror. "So, you're saying...?"

I nodded. "I'm afraid so. The blog's here to stay, and there's nothing either of us can do about it."

Just after five-thirty next morning, I was woken by the sound of the printer in Dad's office. I say "office" but it's actually just a little cupboard where he has his computer and recording equipment. We hang our jackets in there, too, which is usually a good way of muffling the sound of him singing. There was nothing muffled about the printer, though.

52

At first I thought it might be a burglar but I couldn't figure out why a burglar would be using the printer. Maybe they were trying to steal our ink, but if that were the case, surely there were better ways of doing it? I decided to go and investigate.

I rolled out of bed and shuffled on to the landing. The light was on, which made a burglary seem unlikely and I stumbled towards it like a moth. Each eye was operating completely independently, so when one opened, the other closed, as if both halves of my face were taking it in turns to continue sleeping.

"Mum?" I mumbled, squinting in the bright glow of the landing light. Mum was on her knees outside Dad's open office door, several stacks of A4 paper piled up in front of her. She looked up when she heard me and tried to act like she was surprised.

"Oh, Dylan! I didn't wake you, did I?"

"Yes," I said. "You did. What are you doing?"

Mum looked down at the paper, as if seeing it for the first time. "Hmm? Oh, this? Nothing, really. I'm just printing off some campaign leaflets." She laughed falsely. "Since you just happen to have woken up, you can help me."

"Campaign leaflets?" I repeated, my brain still half asleep. "Are you going to be Prime Minister?"

"Not quite. The head of the PTA, remember?" Mum said. She reached into the office-slash-cupboard and pulled out a freshly printed bundle of leaflets. "Once people see these, I'm bound to be voted in."

Mum passed me one of the sheets. It had a photo of her standing in a heroic pose, one foot on top of a pile of paperwork, her eyes gazing off into the middle distance.

VOTE CLAIRE MA
FOR PTA CHAI

SHE'S GREAT

"The paper I'm standing on represents unnecessary expenditure," said Mum. "Or needless bureaucracy, I haven't decided yet."

"Vote Claire Malone for PTA Chair," I read. "She's great."

"Your dad came up with the slogan," said Mum, loading more paper into the printer. "What do you think?"

"It's rubbish," I said.

"Oh. Well. Thanks for that," Mum said. "Turn it over and read the back."

I turned the sheet over. There were three columns of text on the other side. "Wow, that looks boring."

"It's very clever, actually," said Mum. "Fold it up, it's a leaflet. Unfold it and it's a lovely poster for your bedroom wall or window."

"What's going on?" asked Jodie, appearing at her bedroom door.

"Mum's lost the plot," I said.

55

VOTE CLAIRE MALONE
FOR PTA CHAIR

SHE'S GREAT

"I have not!" Mum protested. "I'm just organizing an effective campaign. You don't win elections by lounging around in bed all day."

"It's half five in the morning!" Jodie groaned.

"Yes, well *some* of us have been up since three."

"See?" I said. "Totally lost the plot."

"Your poor father's been driving around all night, trying to buy more paper for the printer." Mum smiled fondly. "That's dedication, that is."

Jodie yawned. "No, he hasn't. He's asleep in the car, I saw him out of my window."

Mum jumped to her feet. "What?!" she cried. "The no-good lazy so-and-so!" She marched along the landing and thundered down the stairs. "You two get folding. I need all those leaflets done before school."

By just before seven, Jodie and I had folded over two thousand leaflets. We did try to point out that there are only seven hundred pupils in our school, but Mum insisted that we keep going, just in case. Just in case of what, she didn't actually say, just "just in case" in general.

Once Mum had woken up Dad – and probably half the street, the way she was shouting – she made him take Destructo for his morning walk as punishment for sleeping in the car instead of going to get her paper.

It was probably just as well that he had. It was only the fact she'd run out of stuff to print on that had made her stop at two thousand leaflets.

It was a shame he wasn't around, actually, as I could have asked him a bit more about the Wagstaffe Cup. He'd gone to the same school as Jodie and me and, although he hadn't been picked for the team, he'd at least witnessed it first-hand.

Today was the first day of events. One of the competition's remaining rules was that the team was selected the day before the contest began, so no one had any time to prepare. The idea was that pupils would study and train harder all year, just in case they were chosen.

Needless to say, this hadn't happened in my case. Because we'd lost every single year, no one at my school really cared about the competition. The kids at Foxley Hill, on the other hand, took it *very* seriously.

"So, the Wagstaffe Cup starts today," I said, as Jodie and I sat eating our toast and cereal. She hadn't been picked for the team when she was in Year Seven, either, but I hoped she might have some inside info, all the same. She made a point of glancing briefly at me, then looking away very deliberately.

"You're not still angry about the blog, are you?"

"Hmm. Let me think," said Jodie, tapping the side of her mouth with her spoon. "YES!"

The hall door opened and Mum swept in. She was wearing a bright blue dress with matching shoes and handbag, and a set of white pearls round her neck. "Well? What do you think?" she said.

"You look like the Queen!" I gasped.

"The Queen's ninety!" said Mum, looking horrified.

"No, I mean the Queen from, like, twenty years ago."

Mum's face darkened.

"Fifty years ago?" I guessed.

"What he means is you look great, Mum," said Jodie. "But why are you dressed like that?"

"I thought I'd walk you both to school today," Mum said.

59

Jodie and I both choked on our breakfast at the same time. "*What?*" I wheezed. "*Why?!*"

"So I can hand out some leaflets for the students to take home to their parents, of course," said Mum.

"I've arranged to meet Dawn this morning, so I can't walk with you, I'm afraid," said Jodie, doing a very good impression of being disappointed. She turned to me, her face crinkling evilly. "Beaky, what about you? Do you have a good reason why Mum can't walk you to school today?"

I swallowed. If my lying powers were ever going to come back, now was the time. I'd never needed them more. *Yes.* That was all I had to say. *Yes.*

"Nope," I said. "There's no reason Mum can't walk me to school."

Aaaaaaaaaaaargh!

"Excellent," said Mum, snatching my half-eaten plate of toast out from under me. "Then hurry up and get dressed. I want to get there early to make sure I see *everyone.*"

CHAPTER 4

THE ASSEMBLY

Mum stepped in front of a group of Year Ten boys and flashed them a toothy grin. "Good morning, gentlemen," she said. "I'm Claire Malone. Dylan's mum."

She pointed over to where I was standing beside the school gates, trying very hard to be invisible.

"As you know, the position of chair of the PTA has become available…"

"The what?" asked one of the boys.

"The PTA," Mum said again, as if that explained everything. When it was clear it didn't, she continued. "The Parent Teacher Association."

"Oh," said one of the boys.

"Aha! *Now* you're interested!" Mum laughed.

"Not really."

"Right," said Mum, doing a very good job of keeping her smile in place. "Well... You'll be delighted to know I'm building my campaign around cutting unnecessary school bureaucracy, and streamlining the process of— Hey ... hang on," said Mum, thrusting flyers into the boys' hands as they hurried past her through the gates.

"I hope I can count on your parents' votes!" she called after them, then she came over to join me. "Well, I think that went rather well."

"It didn't," I said. "They'll just throw them in the bin."

Mum sighed. "Try to be a bit more positive, Dylan!"

I shrugged. "They'll *probably* just throw them in the bin. Is that better?"

Mum let out a loud gasp. Her face tightened,

like she'd just eaten a lemon. "I don't believe it. It's that Green woman! What's *she* doing here?"

I followed her gaze. A woman who looked a lot like Mum was marching towards us. She wore a near-identical outfit, but hers was green, not blue. In her arms was a big stack of leaflets and trudging along beside her was Evie from my class. Of course! Evie Green. I hadn't made the connection between Evie and Mum's arch-nemesis before.

Mrs Green stopped half a metre away from Mum. They eyeballed each other like gunfighters in an old Western.

"Helen."

"Claire."

Evie gave me a wave. "All right, Beaky?"

I shook my head. "Not really."

Evie smiled. "Nah. Nor me. All set for the contest?"

"Not really," I said, shaking my head again.

Evie's smile widened. "Nah. Nor me."

"I didn't think I'd see you here," said Mum. "Never pictured you as an early riser."

"Oh, I've been up since four," said Mrs Green.

Mum smirked. "Three," she said.

"I didn't go to bed until two," said Mrs Green.

"Oh. Well, that explains why you look so *tired*," said Mum. She and Mrs Green glared at each other, their fingers hovering over their respective bundles of leaflets.

At that moment, a Year Eight girl made the mistake of walking past. Mum and Mrs Green both pounced, thrusting their flyers at her and shouting over one another.

"Take this!"

"Give it to your parents!"

"No, take mine!"

"Mine!"

Evie sidled up to me. "Should we leave them to it?"

"Definitely," I said.

"Who do you think is going to win?" Evie asked.

I watched both our mums practically wrestling outside the school. "Dunno," I said. "But it's definitely not going to be us."

Speaking of things we definitely weren't going to win, after registration we all headed to the special assembly that would mark the start of the Winston and Watson Wagstaffe Cup of Competitive Chummery.

Wayne, Chloe, Evie, Theo and I were all made to stand on the stage to the right of Mr Lawson. On the other side of the stage, five students from Foxley Hill School stood snapped to attention in their crisp green blazers. Like our team, Foxley

Hill's was made up of three boys and two girls. Unlike ours, they looked completely confident, as if their victory was already in the bag. Which, to be fair, it probably was.

Two teachers stood next to them, at the end of the line. One was clearly a PE teacher. His whistle was a dead giveaway. He also looked like he was a member of the SAS and probably ran twenty miles every morning before breakfast.

I looked along the stage to my right at Mrs Moir, our PE teacher. She'd been at the school longer than anyone could remember – she'd even taught Dad when he'd been my age – and her hips made a weird clicking noise whenever she walked more than two miles per hour. Despite that, she seemed to be under the impression she was still as fit as she'd been back in the 1970s. Coincidentally, her tracksuit – a bright red nylon atrocity with a single white stripe down each arm – had last been fashionable around about that same decade. It was a mystery why Mr Lawson didn't retire her.

Mrs Moir was also a bit deaf. She was having to lean so far over to hear what Mr Lawson was saying that I was amazed she hadn't fallen flat on her face.

The other teachers involved in the contest were from both schools' English departments. Foxley Hill's Head of English was much younger than any of the teachers at our school. She looked like a sort of funky librarian, with elf-like black hair and thick-rimmed glasses. Our Head of English, on the other hand, looked less like an elf and more like an ogre.

Mr Heft was the largest teacher in school, no matter which direction you measured him in. He'd had to have a special over-sized desk built for him and he had to duck every time he passed through a door.

Our school's assembly hall is pretty tiny and can usually only handle one year group at a time. Today it was busier than I'd ever seen it. Rows of tightly packed chairs stretched all the way from the very front to the back, with an aisle down the middle, splitting the audience in two.

On the left side – our side – the whole of Years Seven and Eight had been squashed in, so there was standing room only at the back. Across the aisle, a hundred or so Foxley Hill School pupils and teachers sat to a sort of hushed attention.

Mr Lawson had been banging on about the history of the contest for a full ten minutes now. He was all "noble tradition" this and "great honour" that, and it was clear from their fidgeting that our half of the audience had lost interest about ten seconds in. The Foxley Hill pupils, on the other hand, were soaking up every word that dropped from Mr Lawson's mouth, as if he were the most fascinating man alive.

"Wow, their head teacher must be *really* boring," I whispered to Theo. "They think Mr Lawson's actually interesting! I mean... *Mr Lawson.*"

I caught Wayne's glare and quietly cleared my throat. "Sorry. Forgot he was your dad."

"The rounds of the contest are the same as always," Mr Lawson announced. "First up is the quiz round, which this year will include a quick-fire spelling segment."

The Foxley Hill pupils murmured excitedly, while most of our supporters sighed and rolled their eyes.

"Then we'll move on to the debating round. Both teams will be given the motion and will have one hour to compose their arguments before delivering them during the debate."

There was a faint smattering of applause from the Foxley Hill side of the audience. Over on our side, someone burped. It echoed impressively around the hall and Mr Lawson had to raise his voice to be heard over the sound of giggling from our school's Year Eights.

"And finally, the main event," Mr Lawson continued, his voice taking on a sort of hushed excitement. "The overnight wilderness survival round. Both teams will be taken to two randomly selected spots in the woodlands behind the school and tasked with making a camp. Then, tomorrow morning, they'll complete an obstacle course and race back here. Whichever team makes it back first will be crowned the victor of that round."

He gestured to his left. "Without any further ado, it gives me great pleasure to introduce the team from Foxley Hill School. In fact, I believe they're going to introduce themselves, is that right, Mr Mann?"

The Foxley Hill PE teacher nodded abruptly. "Yah, is right," he said in a fierce Eastern European accent. He screamed the next few words, making everyone from my school – including Mr Lawson –

jump. "TEAM FOXLEY HILL, GO!"

A tall, pale-looking girl who was at the end of
the line closest to the middle of the
stage immediately launched herself
into a cartwheel from a standing start.
She landed in perfect splits and
raised her arms in the air in a
way that just cried out for a
fanfare noise. It would have been an
impressive move at the Commonwealth
Games and the fact she managed
it wearing full school uniform only
made it more impressive.

"Felicity Swanson," the girl announced. The
Foxley Hill pupils applauded enthusiastically.
Everyone from my school was still staring at her in
disbelief as she stood up, bowed, then returned to
the line.

If we were stunned then – and we were – the
next two minutes were positively shocking. All
along the line, the Foxley Hill kids demonstrated

some sort of amazing acrobatic skill, each one more impressive than the last.

Edgar Knope somersaulted. Christopher Eccles backflipped. Twice. Jessica Kwon somehow managed to somersault and backflip at the same time, landing in a weird crab-position that made it look like her head was on upside down.

 The boy at the far end was last to show off. He was much taller and broader than the rest of his team, towering almost as tall as his hulking PE teacher. He had the wispy beginnings of a moustache and could easily have passed for sixteen.

"Malcolm McQuarrie," he said, in a deep, Scottish-sounding accent. He didn't move and I assumed the acrobatics display must be done, but then he fell forwards into a push-up position, flicked his legs up into the air and spun on his head.

Round and round he went, spinning like a top. The eyes of everyone in the audience followed his dizzying twirl, then even our side applauded when he stopped spinning, placed a hand on the floor, and raised himself up into a single-arm handstand.

"We'll have to do something," Wayne whispered. "We're going to look rubbish if we just wave when our name's called out."

"Do something? Like what?" asked Evie.

"Gymnastics," said Wayne. Across the stage, Malcolm was now balancing on three fingers as he pulled off an impressive mid-air splits. "Like that."

"Oh yeah, no problem," muttered Theo.

"Can you do that stuff, Wayne?" asked Chloe.

Wayne looked flustered, like he always did when Chloe spoke to him. "What? Yeah. That? Deffo. Easy."

Chloe nodded, impressed. "Cool."

"Nah," Wayne shrugged. "It's nothing."

"You should show us, Wayne," said Evie.

73

She nudged me with her elbow. "We'd love to see it, wouldn't we, Beaky?"

"Yeah. I'd love to see it," I agreed.

The audience erupted in a standing ovation as Malcolm finished whatever acrobatic madness he was doing and took a bow. Mr Lawson stared at the Foxley Hill pupils in horrified disbelief until the clapping died away.

I'll be honest, Mr Lawson hadn't looked particularly hopeful before the Foxley Hill mob had introduced themselves but now he looked like a broken man. He gestured vaguely towards our team and mumbled.

"And for our school – Theo, Chloe, Dylan, Evie and Wayne."

At the mention of his name, Wayne shot Chloe an anxious glance, then ran forwards and launched himself into what would actually have been an almost impressive cartwheel, had he not completely misjudged where the end of the stage was.

Rather than land on his feet as he had presumably hoped to, he hurtled off the stage, flipped once in the air, then face-planted with a *thud* on to the wooden floor. As one, everyone from my school stood up, trying to get a better view. They needn't have bothered. Wayne jumped to his feet  immediately, trying to look like everything had gone exactly as planned.

"Ta-daa!" he said shakily. Then, accompanied by the sound of confused, muted applause, he limped back up to join us on the stage.

"Impressive," whispered Evie, and I had to jam my hand into my mouth to stop myself telling Wayne just what I thought of his performance.

In the centre of the stage, Mr Lawson sighed, then made a valiant attempt at smiling. "Well," he said. "May the best team win!"

CHAPTER 5
THE CONTEST BEGINS

After assembly, both teams were taken through to the dining hall to get to know each other a bit before the first round got underway. The four teachers all gathered in one corner, leaving us kids milling about at the other end. The Foxley Hill pupils faced us in a perfect line, their hands behind their backs, vague sneers on their faces.

Nobody was talking, so I decided to break the ice. "All right?" I said, holding a hand out to Malcolm, the boy who looked like he should be in sixth form. "I'm Dylan, but most people call me Beaky."

"No wonder," snorted Malcolm. "Your nose is enormous."

"All the better to smell you with," I said. Malcolm's sneer became a scowl. "I have no idea why I said that," I admitted. "I'm not going to smell you. And if I did, I'm sure you'd be very clean. Fragrant, even."

Theo put an arm round my shoulder. "He's going to shut up now," he said. "Aren't you?"

"Yes, I'm going to shut up now," I agreed, letting him lead me away from Malcolm.

"Here's what's going to happen," said Malcolm. "We're going to win the quiz. We're going to win the debate. We're going to win, full stop."

"Yeah? Well ... you might not," said Wayne, in what was probably the weakest comeback of all time.

The Foxley Hill kids sniggered. Malcolm's face

split into a smug grin. "Oh, and who's going to beat us? Big Nose and Barbie here?" he said, gesturing to me and Chloe in turn.

"Barbie?" said Chloe, looking up from her phone. "What, is that meant to be an insult?"

One of the Foxley Hill girls – Felicity, I think – looked Chloe up and down. "No, just an honest assessment. Barbie doesn't have anything between *her* ears, either."

Chloe was already looking back at her phone. She tore her eyes away again when she realized Felicity was still speaking to her. "Hmm? Did you say something?"

Malcolm sniggered. "So, if she's Barbie, which of you lot is Ken?"

"Raaargh!" Wayne roared as he hurled himself at Malcolm, his fists flying. Theo and I both jumped back in shock. We'd seen Wayne dishing out plenty of beatings, but he'd always made a point of doing it when there were no adults around to see him.

Now, though, he didn't seem to care that there were four teachers standing at the other end of the hall. He slammed his shoulder into Malcolm's stomach, sending him staggering.

"Take that back!" Wayne hissed. "She's *way* smarter than Barbie!"

"Wayne Lawson!" bellowed Mr Heft. His voice was just as big as the rest of him and seemed to expand to fill the whole hall.

Mr Mann, the Foxley Hill PE teacher, hurtled towards us like an Olympic sprinter. He caught Wayne by the back of his jumper and pulled him away from Malcolm. Mr Heft and Miss Garden, the Foxley Hill English teacher, were next, with Mrs Moir wheezing and panting along behind.

"What do you think you're doing?" Mr Heft demanded, in a voice that shook plaster dust from the ceiling.

"He started it, sir!" said Wayne. "He was insulting –"
Wayne glanced back at Chloe – "our team."

"So you thought you'd beat him up?" said Mr Heft.

"Ha! I'd like to see him try," said Malcolm.

"That's enough from you, Malcolm," said Miss Garden.

"Yes, Miss," said Malcolm, like a trained dog responding to a command.

"I'm very … disappointed," panted Mrs Moir, leaning on Mr Heft for support. She looked like she was about to pass out from the effort of running the length of the hall.

"He must be punished, yes?" said Mr Mann. He punched a fist into the opposite palm. "Punished good."

Mr Heft and Mrs Moir exchanged a glance. "Well, I don't know if that's strictly necessary."

"He assaulted me!" Malcolm pointed out. "He should be disqualified."

Panic flashed across our teachers' faces. "Now, I don't think we need go that far," said Mr Heft. "How about he misses the first part of the competition?"

"What!" Wayne spluttered. "But that's the quiz. I'm supposed to be doing the spelling. I'm the best speller we've got."

"Beaky could do it," suggested Evie. "You're pretty good at spelling, aren't you, Beaky?"

"Um … compared to who?" I asked.

Evie shrugged. "Dunno, I just sort of thought you'd be good at that stuff."

Mrs Moir shot Mr Mann a pleading look. "Would that do? If we exclude Wayne from the spelling round?"

"He really is our best speller," said Mr Heft. "By quite some distance. I think losing him for the round would be punishment enough."

Mr Mann considered the suggestion for a few agonizing moments, then shrugged. "Very well. This will do."

"Great!" said Mr Heft. "Great news. And Wayne, we'll have a serious chat about this later, understood?"

"Yes, sir," Wayne muttered, then we all looked round as the dining-hall door opened and Mr Lawson popped his head in.

"Ready?" he said.

The Foxley Hill pupils all formed a circle and stretched their hands into the middle. Everyone watched as they performed some elaborate gesture, which involved a lot of hand-slapping, knuckle-bumping and the odd bit of finger-waggling. Once all that was out of the way, they raised their outstretched arms over their heads.

"Foxley Hill *ready!*" they all cheered in note-perfect unison.

Mr Lawson tried very hard to keep his smile on his face. "Right. Good," he said, then he looked at us. "Ready?"

I looked at the others. We all shrugged. "Not really," I admitted. "But I suppose we'll give it a go."

Twenty minutes later, things weren't exactly going *great* but we were in better shape than pretty much anyone had been expecting. Especially me.

Theo and Chloe had done the general knowledge round for our team and we'd hit an amazing lucky streak by getting four different questions related to bus and coach design of the late twentieth century. Theo – secret bus-spotter that he was – had buzzed in with the correct answers before Mr Lawson had even finished asking the questions, and while we finished the round a few points behind Foxley Hill, we'd come pretty close to holding our own.

"Well, then," said Mr Lawson. "That was exciting, wasn't it?"

The Foxley Hill pupils certainly seemed to think so, breaking into thrilled applause as the victorious Christopher and Jessica stood and took a bow, then left the stage. On the other side of the hall, our Year Sevens and Eights barely seemed to be paying any attention at all. Mr Lawson raised his voice and changed his tone to make it clear that they should start listening pretty sharpish.

"And now, the spelling segment of the quiz round," he announced. "Felicity and Wayne will be going head to head."

Mr Heft leaned in from the wings. "Actually, Mr Lawson, Dylan will be taking Wayne's place."

An expression of absolute horror spread across Mr Lawson's face like a rash. "What? Why?"

"Long story. I'll explain later," said Mr Heft.

84

Mr Lawson sighed, then glanced towards the wings and gestured for me to come on to the stage. "Good luck, Beaky," said Evie, patting my shoulder.

"Don't let the fact that there are hundreds of people watching and silently judging you put you off," added Theo, as I shuffled past him and Chloe on to the stage and took my place behind the buzzer.

"Thanks for that," I groaned.

Wayne didn't say anything – he just glared.

Felicity from Foxley Hill stood behind the buzzer on their side of the stage, her back straight and her head held high. She looked way more confident than I felt. Then again, if she'd been hugging herself on the floor and crying, she'd probably still have looked more confident than I felt.

I'm not the worst speller in Year Seven but I'm far from the best. I've pretty much got the hang of the "i before e" thing but that's about all I've got the hang of and everything else is just sort of guesswork. I had a feeling Felicity wouldn't need to guess at all.

"OK, so this is a quick-fire round," said Mr Lawson. "I'll state the word, then whoever buzzes in first gets a chance to answer. If they get it wrong, it'll be passed over to the other team to answer. Understood?"

"Understood," said Felicity.

"Yep. Got it," I said.

"Then here we go. Good luck, both," said Mr Lawson. He lifted a card and read from it. "Can you spell *onomatopoeia*?"

I slammed my hand down on the buzzer.

Mr Lawson looked at Felicity first, then turned to me in amazement when he realized I'd been the one to buzz in. "Dylan?"

"No," I said.

Mr Lawson frowned. "I'm sorry?"

"No, I can't spell onomatopoeia."

The head blinked slowly. "Oh. Um. Right. Well, why did you buzz in?"

I shifted uncomfortably on the spot. "Because

you asked if I could spell it, and I felt like I should give you an honest answer."

The fact I'd buzzed in had taken even me by surprise. I knew I had no idea how to spell the word but when Mr Lawson had asked if I could, the urge to tell the truth had been too strong to fight.

Mr Lawson looked at me for what felt like quite a long time, then turned to Felicity. "Foxley Hill?"

"O-N-O-M-A-T-O-P-O-E-I-A," said Felicity. She gave a curt little nod at the end, like she knew it was right before Mr Lawson had even confirmed it.

"Correct!" said Mr Lawson. "Now, next question, fingers on buzzers. Can you spell *bureaucracy*?"

BZZT! My hand slammed down on the button again all by itself.

"No."

Mr Lawson's face darkened. Behind him, our half of the audience began to snigger and giggle. "I'm not being cheeky, sir," I insisted. "I'm just answering the question."

87

"Well don't!" said Mr Lawson. "If you don't know how to spell it, don't buzz in!"

I kept my mouth shut while Mr Lawson passed the word over to Felicity. She, of course, got it right. Mr Lawson flicked to the next card and shot me a warning look. "Right. Next one. Remember, only buzz in if you know it. Understood?"

"Understood," I said. I could feel Wayne's gaze burning into me from the wings and I didn't dare turn round to look.

Mr Lawson cleared his throat.

I held my breath.

The audience waited.

"Can you spell…" He glanced my way. His eyes narrowed. "*Dodecahedron?*"

BZZZZZZZZT!

I stared at my hand in horror. It was pressing down on the button, making the buzzer ring. I yanked it away and the sound faded into an expectant silence.

I could feel all eyes in the hall on me. Watching. Waiting. Mr Lawson exhaled slowly through his nose. "Dylan," he said, in a way that made my name sound like a bad word. "Do you know how to spell dodecahedron?"

I glanced back at my teammates in the wings. Theo and Evie nodded encouragingly. Wayne glared at me, his face a sort of reddish-purple with rage. Chloe was taking a photo of me on her phone, probably to stick on Instagram – hashtag *spellingfail*.

"Um," I began, turning back to Mr Lawson. "I know it's got a *d* in it. Does that get me half a point?"

CHAPTER 6

ONE-NIL

When the spelling bit finished, I walked off the stage to the sound of stunned silence, then had to listen to the roar of applause for Felicity. Felicity hadn't just won, she'd completely destroyed me. There had been ten words in all and I'd buzzed in first on all ten, only to confirm that I had no idea how to spell any of them.

Mr Lawson had grown increasingly annoyed by my performance but with everyone watching he'd had to keep his temper under control. His face was a dark purple by the time we reached question six, and when I buzzed in for the tenth time, I'm sure I saw him crying.

"Well," I said, joining my teammates. "That could've gone better."

"*Could've gone better?*" Wayne hissed. "That's an understatement! How could it *possibly* have gone any worse?"

I had to admit, ten–nil was pretty much as bad as it could've got, points-wise. Still, there were other ways it could have been worse.

"I suppose ... a lion could've jumped on stage," I said.

Wayne, Chloe and Evie all blinked at the same time. Only Theo didn't seem surprised by the remark.

"What?" said Wayne.

"That would've been worse," I said. "If we'd all been eaten by a lion. Or if the floor had turned to lava. Or if monkeys had—"

Wayne slammed a hand into my chest and

grabbed me by my school tie. His face was suddenly right in mine, his teeth bared. "You think this is a joke, Beaky?"

I frantically shook my head. Theo stepped up beside me. "Hey, leave him alone, Wayne."

"Yeah, he tried his best," said Evie, appearing at my other side. "Why do you even care?"

"I don't," Wayne said. "They can win every round, I don't care."

"He's lying," I wheezed. "You can see it in his eyes."

BZZT Wayne's grip tightened. His fist drew back.

Behind him, Chloe giggled. "It *was* pretty funny, though. *Bzzt.* 'No.' *Bzzt.* 'No.' I was like, *OMG, this is hilarious!*" *BZZT*

Confusion swept across Wayne's face. He released his grip and forced a laugh. "What? I mean, yeah. Yeah, it was pretty funny." His teeth ground together. "Nice one, Beaky," he growled.

I straightened the front of my shirt and had

just begun to relax when Mr Heft came clomping up the steps into the wings. "What on *Earth* was that about?" he demanded, his massive eyes glaring out at me from the centre of his enormous face. "You've probably just lost us the competition!"

"To be fair, sir, we were already behind," said Theo.

"And that girl was amazing at spelling," added Evie.

"And it's Wayne's fault for trying to punch Malcolm," I said. "Also, we're rubbish and were pretty much guaranteed to lose, anyway," I concluded, which didn't really help matters.

"Still, I thought we'd taught you better than that, Dylan," Mr Heft said. "I mean, some of those words you should've known in Year Five!"

"Yeah, I know, sir, that's what I told him," said Theo. I stared at him in shock. Was my best friend about to betray me? "We've been standing here

93

arguing about how to spell 'onomatopoeia', and he refuses to accept he's wrong. Can you spell it for us now, sir?"

Mr Heft swallowed. "Hmm?"

Evie smirked. "Yeah, sir," she said, joining in. "Can you spell 'onomatopoeia' so we can settle the argument once and for all?"

Mr Heft nodded his massive head. "Yep. Definitely. No problem," he said. He opened his mouth to start, then frowned. He reached into his pocket and took out his mobile. "Sorry, I'd better get this," he said, pointing to the completely silent phone. Then he hurried back down the steps, jumped the last two, and ducked through the door at the bottom.

"Thanks," I said.

"No problem," said Theo.

"Any time," added Evie, patting me on the shoulder. Theo looked at her, then at me, then at her, then back to me again. His jaw dropped.

"What?" I asked, but Theo just shook his head.

"Oh, nothing," he said. "I'll tell you later."

"I don't think he could really spell it," said Chloe, pointing with her thumb in the direction Mr Heft had fled. "That onomappy-thingy. I don't think he could spell it. It's lucky for him his phone rang when it did."

We all looked at her in silence for a moment, trying to figure out if she was joking. After a while, we all came to the conclusion that she probably wasn't.

"Yeah. Really lucky," said Theo. He started to roll his eyes but then caught Wayne glowering at him, so pretended he was going to look up at the ceiling instead. "That could do with a paint," he said, avoiding Wayne's glare.

Suddenly Mr Lawson's voice echoed from the stage. "I'd now like to invite both teams to join me on the stage once more!"

"Oh no, what now?" I groaned.

"Second round," said Wayne. "It's the debate."

"Do I have to do anything?" I asked.

Wayne snorted. "You? No chance. You'll blow it again. We need three people for this round and you're not going to be one of them."

"Hooray!" I cheered, raising my hands in celebration. I led the team out on to the stage, confident I could safely ignore anything that Mr Lawson was going to say.

On the other side of the stage, Mr Mann and Mrs Moir were half carrying, half dragging a huge scoreboard from behind the side curtain. Mrs Moir grunted and sweated as she heaved it across the stage. Mr Mann, meanwhile, carried his end with one hand.

"It is good here, yah?" Mr Mann barked, with such ferocity I thought poor Mrs Moir was going to have a heart attack.

"Yes, there's fine," said Mr Lawson. He watched, dejectedly, as Mr Mann adjusted the numbers until the scoreboard read:

NUTLEY GRANGE: 0
FOXLEY HILL: 1

The PE teachers left the stage and Mr Lawson turned back to the audience. "There's still everything to play for!" he said, but he didn't sound convinced. "Up next, we have the debate round. Three members of each team will debate a randomly selected issue, with points awarded for style, delivery and content."

He reached under his lectern and pulled out a bowl filled with lots of little pieces of paper. "These are all the suggestions made by students, parents, staff and even members of the public via the contest's website. There were some *interesting suggestions* this year," he said, glaring out at our school's Year Eights. "But we've carefully vetted each suggestion and narrowed the list down to ensure we get a great topic both teams can really get their teeth into."

"Wait, what are we getting our teeth into?" whispered Chloe, who had been paying even less attention than I had. "We don't have to eat anything, do we?"

"No, he didn't mean our actual teeth, it's not an eating contest," Evie assured her. "It's a metaphor."

"That's a relief," said Chloe. "I thought it was going all *I'm a Celebrity, Get Me Out of Here!* for a minute there, and there's *no way* I'm eating caterpillars or crocodile tongues or whatever."

Mr Lawson shook the bowl to mix up the paper. "Now, I'm going to invite Miss Garden to come up and choose the motion."

There was enthusiastic applause from the Foxley Hill team and their half of the audience as the elf-like English teacher came trotting on to the stage. She waved out at the crowd, then reached a hand into the bowl, fished out a piece of paper and handed it to Mr Lawson.

"Thank you, Miss Garden," said Mr Lawson, ushering her back to her seat. He unfolded the piece of paper. "Here's the subject for our debate. It has been submitted online by a member of the public. One 'M. Shirley'."

My head snapped up. Theo turned to look at me. "M. Shirley?" he whispered. "Could that be...?"

"Madame Shirley!" I said. I shook my head. "No. No, I mean ... what are the chances?"

Mr Lawson took a sip of water, then cleared his throat. "The motion the teams will be debating today, is..." He paused dramatically.

"Come on!" I yelped. "It's not *The X Factor*. Hurry up and read what it says!"

The head teacher glared at me, but then began to read. Each word that came out of his mouth sent little electric tingles of shock through me, but it was the last one that nearly made my hair stand on end.

"It is always best to tell the truth."

I gasped. It was her! It had to be! Madame Shirley herself, the crazy old woman who had stolen my lying powers, must have sent in that suggestion.

"Arguing in favour of the motion will be the Foxley Hill team," said Mr Lawson. "While the Nutley Grange team will be arguing against. Both teams have one hour to decide who will be speaking for them and to prepare their arguments."

As Mr Lawson dismissed us all, I spun to face Wayne. "You've got to let me take part!" I said. "I can do this. I'll be great at this one!"

"No chance," said Wayne. "You completely blew that last round. There's no way I'm giving you another chance. Me, Chloe and Evie will do it."

"But listen!" I protested. "I promise I'll be *brilliant* at this. I think a weird old woman wants me to take part," I babbled. "I think that's why she sent in the suggestion!"

Everyone, with the exception of Theo, looked at me as if I'd lost my mind. "What are you talking about?" Wayne demanded.

"The mad old woman who broke my brain!" I blurted, as if that explained everything. "With her truth-telling machine!"

Chloe looked me up and down. "Is he having some sort of breakdown?"

"Honestly, he'd be really good at this one," said Theo. "You should give him a chance."

"No!" Wayne spat. "I'm team captain and I decide who's doing what."

"Who says you're team captain?" Theo asked.

Wayne turned round and shoved a fist right in his face. "This says so, all right?" he growled. Then, when it was clear Theo wasn't going to argue any further, he gave a nod. "Right, ladies, let's go and get working on our arguments. We'll give this Foxley Hill mob something to chew on."

Chloe looked worried. "Chew on?"

"Relax, it won't be locusts or bits of kangaroo," Evie said. She shot me a smile, then followed the other two down the steps and out into the corridor.

Theo waited until they were out of earshot before speaking. "She well fancies you."

"Who, Chloe?"

"No! Not Chloe. Evie," Theo said.

I shook my head and laughed. "What? No she doesn't."

"She definitely does," Theo argued. "Did you see the way she kept looking at you and leaping to your defence all the time?"

"*You* leap to my defence all the time," I pointed out.

"Yeah, but that's because I'm your best mate,

so I have to. It's the law. She doesn't though. She does it because she fancies you."

"No, she doesn't fancy me," I said, then I pointed to my mouth. "And because I said that, it must be true, because I can't lie."

"Yeah, but that just means you don't *believe* she fancies you," Theo said, smirking. "But you'll see, Beaky. You'll see..."

CHAPTER 7

ARGUMENTS

Theo and I sat at the back of a classroom, keeping out of Wayne's way. He was at the front of the class, Chloe on one side, Evie on the other. They were hard at work trying to come up with their speeches and although I'd offered to help, Wayne had requested that I didn't get involved.

"Keep your big nose out of it, Beaky!" had been his exact words, in case you were wondering.

Theo and I had tried to pass the time by playing Rock, Paper, Scissors but I couldn't stop myself announcing which one I was going to choose before each round, so we'd given up pretty quickly.

"I Spy?" asked Theo.

I shrugged. "Yeah, OK."

"You go first."

I looked around the room. "I spy with my little eye … a desk."

Theo shook his head. "No, that's not how you play it. You say the first letter."

"I know," I said. I looked around the room a second time. "I spy with my little eye … a chair."

I slapped myself on the forehead. "Argh! I can't even play I Spy! How can that possibly count as lying?"

"I suppose it's a bit like keeping a secret," Theo said, "and you're not very good at that."

"Theo was born with six nipples!" I shouted, then I clamped my hand over my mouth. "No," I mumbled. "It isn't one of my strong points."

"Keep it down," Wayne barked. "We're trying to practise our speeches here."

"How come you care so much, anyway?" asked Theo.

Wayne shifted in his seat. "What? I don't care. Why would I care? It's stupid."

"Yes, you do," I said. "It's obvious."

Wayne sighed and drummed his fingers on the desk in front of him. "So? What if I do? No one from this school has ever won the contest before. The Foxley Hill teachers are always making fun of my dad. And, I dunno, I just want to beat them."

I gasped. "Wayne Lawson, you actually have emotions like a proper human being. We'll make a real live boy of you yet!"

"Shut up, Beaky," Wayne growled.

"Look, if you want to win, let me help with the speeches!" I said, jumping up. "Seriously, I'm like the world's leading expert on telling the truth! The subject was literally sent in just for me!"

"Sit down and shut up," Wayne warned. "You're not doing it. We don't need you, anyway. We've got it all sorted, haven't we, girls?"

Chloe looked up from her phone. "Hmm?"

"The debate," said Wayne. "We've got it all in hand."

Chloe's perfectly shaped eyebrows knotted. "Debate?"

"Yes," said Wayne, trying to keep his smile fixed in place. "I gave you your speech just a minute ago, remember?"

Chloe peered down at a sheet of paper in front of her. "Oh, so you did! So I just read this, do I?"

"That's the idea," said Evie.

Chloe shrugged. "Oh, then yeah, it'll be fine."

"Wayne, trust me on this…" I began to protest, but then the classroom door opened and Mr Heft squeezed through the gap.

"Right then, time's up," he said. "We're all waiting."

"For what?" asked Chloe. Evie waved the paper under her nose again. "Oh, the debate. Right."

"We're counting on you here," said Mr Heft. "*I'm* counting on you." He shot me a glare. "After that spelling round... Well, let's just say, my reputation is on the line."

"And your job, probably," I added.

"Yes, thank you for that, Dylan," Mr Heft muttered.

"When do you want to speak, Chloe?" Wayne asked.

Chloe thought for a moment. "I don't mind. I'll go anywhere. Not first, though. I'd rather not go first. Or last. Anywhere but first or last."

"So ... second, basically?" said Evie.

"Yes. That's perfect!"

108

The three of them got to their feet and we all headed for the door. "OK, I'll open, Chloe will go next, then Evie can close," said Wayne.

"What about us?" asked Theo. "What will we do?"

Wayne narrowed his eyes. "Stay here and keep out of our way," he growled. "Both of you!"

The next half hour passed very slowly. Theo and I sat in the empty classroom, listening to the droning of voices and regular bursts of applause echoing along the corridor from the hall. The voices were muffled, so we couldn't hear what was being said, but judging by the levels of clapping, one team was doing much better than the other.

"Three guesses who's winning," said Theo.

"But there are only two teams," I pointed out.

"Oh, yeah. Fair point," Theo admitted. "Two guesses, then."

"That still means I'm one hundred per cent guaranteed to get it right."

"Fine! Forget it, I just meant we're probably losing," said Theo.

"Well, yeah," I agreed. "But you never know. We might not be."

The classroom door opened and Mrs Moir creaked in. "We're losing," she announced. "It's not pretty."

"See?" said Theo. "Told you."

Mrs Moir stepped aside and Evie shuffled in, clutching at her stomach and groaning. "In you go, pet," said Mrs Moir. "You take a seat."

"Hey, what's up, Evie?" I asked.

"Poor thing has a tummy ache," said Mrs Moir before Evie could answer. "Nerves, probably. It's her turn to speak next. Theo, Wayne wants you to stand in."

I looked over at Evie just as she sat down. She winked at me, then went back to groaning. My hand shot up.

"I'll do it!"

Mrs Moir turned to Theo. "Is that OK with you?"

"I insist," said Theo. He clapped me on the back. "Knock 'em dead, Beaky."

I hurried for the door, flashing Evie a grateful smile on the way past. "Follow me," said Mrs Moir. "And try to keep up if you can!" She set off towards the hall at a snail's pace.

"Tell you what, I'll go on ahead and you catch up," I said, strolling past her. I took the steps leading up to the stage two at a time and stumbled through the curtain just as the beam of a spotlight hit me in the face.

"Dylan," groaned Mr Lawson from somewhere in the blinding glare.

"Beaky!" hissed Wayne, sounding even less pleased than his dad. "I told Mrs Moir to send

Theo. Now we're *bound* to lose."

I blinked away the glare and saw Evie's empty chair just ahead of me. Still a little dazzled, I sat down.

"It's your turn," Wayne growled. "Stand up."

I stood up. On the other side of the stage, three Foxley Hill pupils sniggered behind their hands.

"Did you prepare any notes?" Mr Lawson asked.

"No," I said. "None."

Mr Lawson gripped the edges of his lectern like he might be about to collapse. He raised his eyes to the ceiling and muttered something under his breath. I didn't hear what it was but I could guess it probably wasn't anything complimentary.

"Would you like a minute to read Evie's notes?" he asked.

I glanced down at the notepad sitting on the desk in front of me. I lifted the cover, expecting to see a load of scribbled arguments, but instead found just two words written on the front page.

Good Luck!

I quickly closed the notepad again. "No, I'm fine," I said. "I'll just make it up as I go along."

Mr Lawson and Wayne both groaned in perfect unison. "Are you *sure* about that, Dylan?" the head teacher asked. "We can give you a minute or two."

"No," I said. "No, I'm fine."

"Sure?" said Mr Lawson, his voice coming out as a high-pitched squeak. "Final answer?"

"Final answer," I said. I cleared my throat. "Ladies and gentlemen," I began, but Mr Lawson interrupted me.

"You have to come and stand up here. We've only got one microphone," he said, gesturing to his lectern.

"Oh, right, sorry," I said. I crossed the stage, accompanied by more sniggering from the Foxley Hill pupils.

Mr Lawson stood his ground at the lectern. "Dylan will be arguing against the motion that it is always best to tell the truth," he said. He still didn't move aside.

"Um, can I get past?" I asked.

"Hmm?"

"The microphone," I said. "I need it to speak."

"Yes. Yes, of course," Mr Lawson said. Taking a deep breath, he released his grip on the lectern and shuffled a few awkward steps backwards.

I approached the microphone and leaned in. My mouth had gone dry and I suddenly felt very self-conscious. The whole audience was staring at me in expectant silence. "All right?" I said, then a screech of feedback echoed around the hall.

"Not so close," Mr Lawson said.

I moved my head back a little.

I swallowed.

"I'm going to tell you a story," I said.

And then, I began my speech.

CHAPTER 8

THE BIG SPEECH

When it came to stories about the consequences of telling the truth, I had plenty to choose from. I could have talked about almost breaking up my aunt and uncle's relationship, the beatings my truth-telling had earned me from Jodie, the trouble I'd got into at school – any of it.

But I didn't talk about any of the stuff that had happened as a result of Madame Shirley's truth-telling machine. Those stories were all *good*, don't get me wrong. They'd have helped my side's argument, no doubt about it.

But there was another story from way back that I knew wouldn't just help our argument. It would win it.

"When I was little, we had a neighbour called Mrs Munn," I said. "She was old. About … eighty, I think. She was nice, though, not all mean and grumpy like a lot of old people can be."

Behind me, I heard Wayne whisper. "What's he on about? He's supposed to be talking about telling the truth."

"One year, when I was about six, Mrs Munn asked me what I wanted for Christmas. She always bought me and Jodie Christmas presents. She was nice like that. I told her I wanted a *Power Rangers* action figure and I showed her a picture of it. I even told her which shop to get it from. 'No problem,' she said. 'Leave it to me.'"

"Is this going somewhere?" Mr Lawson hissed but I ignored him.

"Christmas morning came. Mrs Munn popped round with her presents – one for Jodie, one for me and a box of sweets for my mum and dad. I prodded at my present and it was suspiciously soft. I could tell right away it wasn't a Power Ranger. But she smiled at me and looked all hopeful. It was quite sweet, actually, in a really old and wrinkled kind of way." I looked up and, to my amazement, the entire audience was watching me intently, hanging on my every word.

"So, I opened it. It was a pair of pants. A pair of extra-large, navy blue men's Y-fronts to be precise and I'm not even convinced they were new!" I said, and a ripple of laughter murmured through the audience.

"I turned to her and I remember she looked so worried, so ... nervous. And then she said, 'I hope that's what you asked for. My memory isn't very good these days.'"

The audience fell completely silent. Even the Foxley Hill team were holding their breath.

"And I said, 'Thank you, Mrs Munn. This is just what I've always wanted.' And she smiled. This huge smile of, like, *relief*. Like ... like she'd got it right, you know?"

I took a deep breath. "This might be the most embarrassing thing I ever say, but that smile ... that was the best Christmas present I ever got."

I looked out across the audience. I'd expected that announcement to be met by humiliating laughter and a tidal wave of name-calling, but no one spoke. A few of our Year Sevens wiped their eyes on their sleeves. Even the Year Eights looked like they'd been moved by the story.

It was the perfect moment. For about five seconds.

"Obviously, it was a lie," I said. "If I'd been telling the truth, I'd have said, 'Hey, Mrs Munn's lost her marbles – stick her in the nuthouse.'"

The audience laughed at that. I think I even heard Mr Lawson chuckle. "I told a lie and it meant an old woman didn't have her Christmas ruined.

People think lying's bad but it isn't. Lying is what makes the world go round," I said. I pointed to a random kid in our side of the audience.

"Imagine you walked into class tomorrow and told Miss Knox about her terrible breath. She'd kill you. Probably by breathing on you."

The boy I'd pointed to giggled nervously and nodded.

My arm swept right, finding a girl in Year Eight who had a reputation for causing trouble in class. "Imagine the teachers all told you what they actually think of you? They'd probably get fired."

"Hey!" she protested, then she shrugged. "Yeah, fair enough."

"'No, I don't mind.' 'No, it's not a problem, really.' 'No, that new haircut is great!' We lie all the time, and more often than not it's to make someone else feel good, or to make their day go a little more smoothly," I said. "Take that ability to lie away and everything falls apart."

I knew my time had nearly run out, so I wrapped

up my speech. "Is it important to tell the truth sometimes? Yes, of course! But always? Brutal honesty twenty-four hours a day, seven days a week? Nothing good can come of that. Trust me."

I did a little bow to complete and utter silence. "Uh, that's me done," I said.

From somewhere behind me there came the sound of a single person clapping. It sounded embarrassingly faint in the vast, cavernous hall.

I turned to find out who it was and was surprised to see Wayne getting to his feet. Beside him, Chloe began to clap, too, then I spotted Theo and Evie lurking in the wings. They both gave me a thumbs up, then joined in the applause.

The sound began to spread. First some of our Year Sevens started to clap, then the Year Eights joined in. To my amazement, it even leaped the aisle to the other side of the hall. In just a few moments, the whole audience was on its feet, clapping and whooping and cheering.

Mr Lawson stepped up to the lectern. I swear there was a tear in the corner of his eyes as he placed a hand on my shoulder. "Mrs Munn will be very proud," he said.

"Oh, no, she's dead," I told him. "She was hit by a bus when I was eight. Twice, actually."

"*Twice?*"

"It reversed."

Mr Lawson's face fell. "Right. Oh, I see. Well... Good job, anyway."

I returned to my seat with the applause ringing in my ears. "That was, like, totally awesome," said Chloe, not glancing up from her phone. She finished tapping on her screen. "Hashtag MrsMunn," she said. "Boom! You're on Instagram!"

"Um ... good?" I said. I glanced past her to Wayne. He gave me the briefest of brief nods and something that might, if studied under a microscope, be a smile.

Across the stage, the Foxley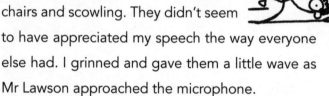
Hill team were leaning back in their
chairs and scowling. They didn't seem
to have appreciated my speech the way everyone
else had. I grinned and gave them a little wave as
Mr Lawson approached the microphone.

"Now that the speeches have concluded, the
teachers will retire to deliberate over their decision,"
said the head. "There will be a short break, then
the winner of this round will be declared."

The Foxley Hill team stood up and huddled in a
circle, taking it in turns to shoot a dirty look my way
every few seconds.

"Beaky, you're *amazing*!" said Evie as she and
Theo hurried out of the wings. She glanced around
at the others. "Your speech was amazing, I mean.
Where did that come from?"

"My mouth," I said. It was the truthful answer but it sounded a little mean when I said it, so I smiled and shrugged and hoped she didn't take offence. I caught Theo grinning at me. "What?" I asked.

Theo rocked on his heels, still smiling. "Oh, nothing," he said, then he gestured to Evie with his eyes and nodded his head very deliberately.

A few minutes later, Mr Lawson returned to the stage. He practically sprinted up the steps, his face lit up with excitement. Wayne, Chloe and I all took our seats, while Theo and Evie stood behind us, leaning on the back of our chairs.

"I think we won," Wayne whispered, watching his dad bounce happily from foot to foot. "I don't believe it. We actually won!"

"You think?" I said. "I find that very hard to believe. From next door, it sounded like you two were completely rubbish."

Chloe looked up from her phone. "Rubbish at what?"

"The debate," I said.

Chloe's brow furrowed. "Debate?"

"The talking thing you did a minute ago," I said.

"Oh," said Chloe. "Yeah, we were terrible."

"No, you weren't," said Wayne, but his heart wasn't in it. Judging by his face, she must've been awful.

"Well, that didn't take long, did it?" Mr Lawson said, barely able to contain his excitement. "It was quite an easy decision in the end." He let out a high-pitched laugh and hopped around on the spot.

"Are you going to wet yourself, sir?" I said. To my amazement, he didn't get angry.

"Not quite, Dylan, but I'm very pleased to report that after the debate round, both teams are now neck and neck with one point each!"

Across the stage, the Foxley Hill mob looked furious.

"We could win this. We could actually win this," said Wayne, watching Mrs Moir shuffling over to update the scoreboard.

And there, in that moment, I started to believe he might even be right. We had drawn level with Foxley Hill for the first time in our school's history. It was still all to play for and I suddenly had the feeling that we were unstoppable, like there was nothing we couldn't do!

It was a feeling that wouldn't last long.

CHAPTER 9

INTO THE WOODS

After lunch, and after changing into the outdoor gear we'd been able to cobble together from the school supply cupboard, Theo, Evie, Chloe, Wayne and me stood at the edge of the forest near our school, listening to Mr Heft going over the safety checks. I say "listening" but we weren't, really. Instead, we were looking up the track a little, where the Foxley Hill team were all gearing up.

"Check out their equipment," said Theo, as the other school slipped their arms into their expensive-looking rucksacks. "It's way better than ours."

I looked down at the stuff our school had given us. One of my walking boots was bigger than the other and the rucksacks had so many holes in them they almost looked like nets.

"To be fair, it couldn't really be any *worse* than ours," I pointed out.

"Are you listening, lads?" said Mr Heft, looming over us like the massive giant he is.

"Yes, sir," said Theo.

"Not even a little bit," I said.

Mr Heft tutted and shook his head. "Right, well, *as I was saying*, this final round is the most difficult of all. Both teams will be dropped at a spot in the woods and have to use their map and compass to find a hidden flag. Once each team has found their flag, they'll then have to navigate to their campsite, light a campfire and settle in for the night."

"Do we have tents?" asked Evie.

"Yes, they're already set up and waiting for you," said Mr Heft. "They're a bit … tired, but they'll do. Tomorrow morning, an alarm will go off in each camp and both teams will then have to navigate quickly to the obstacle course in the middle of the woods, complete it, then run to the finish line with your flag."

He put his immense hands on his even more immense hips. "Any questions?"

I put my hand up. Mr Heft sighed.

"Yes, Dylan?"

"Do these woods have giant bears in them?"

"No, Dylan."

I put my hand down.

I raised it again.

"Yes, Dylan?"

"Do these woods have normal-sized bears in them?"

"No, Dylan. They don't have any bears. Or tigers. Or leopards. Or anything else."

"Squirrels?" I said.

"Well, yes, they might have squirrels, I suppose." Mr Heft shook his head, like he was annoyed at himself for getting involved in this conversation. "Anyway, the point is, it's all very safe. The teachers from both schools won't be far away and you can always reach us on the walkie-talkies if you come across any problems." He raised a finger. "Although, if you do use the walkie-talkies, you'll forfeit the round."

"And why can't we have our phones?" asked Chloe. Mr Lawson had made us leave our mobiles back at the school, safely locked in his desk drawer. Chloe was already pale and twitching.

"Because then you'd all just use GPS and cheat," said Mr Heft. He looked me up and down. "Not that you'll need to cheat with Dylan on the team. This will be a walk in the park for you," he grinned, looking straight at me.

"Hmm?" I said.

"You know, what with your survival skills and everything?"

129

I frowned. "Survival skills?"

"Yes," said Mr Heft. "You told us all about it at the start of the year. About that time you were washed overboard from a ferry when you were nine and had to spend three weeks surviving in the wild."

I laughed. "Ah, yes! I remember saying that now," I said. I braced myself, knowing full well what was about to come out of my mouth. Mr Heft had seemed really impressed when I told him about the three weeks I spent living wild after the incident with the ferry. But he would probably go ballistic when he found out I'd made the whole thing up.

Which was a shame, because he was about to find out right now.

"You see, the thing is, though..." I began.

"He doesn't like to talk about it," said Theo, stepping in front of me. "It brings back bad memories."

"Oh, right. Yes, of course," said Mr Heft.

He passed me a little plastic folder containing a map and compass. "Still, since it seems no one else on the team can read a map or use a compass, I'm putting you in charge."

"Him? He's not in charge," said Wayne. "I'm in charge!"

"Oh, thank God for that," I said, trying to pass him the folder. He didn't take it.

"And since I'm in charge, I've decided that you can do the map-reading. I'll look after the walkie-talkie," Wayne said, taking the handset from Mr Heft and clipping it to his belt.

"Right, I'll hike with you to the starting point, then you're on your own," said the teacher.

"Where's Mrs Moir?" asked Evie.

"She's, er, looking after the minibus," Mr Heft said.

"Do you mean she's sleeping in it, sir?" I asked.

"Possibly," Mr Heft admitted. "She's had a lot of excitement for one day. But she'll meet you at the obstacle course in the morning."

"At the speed she walks, she'd better set off now," I said.

"Very funny, Dylan," said Mr Heft, although the expression on his face suggested it wasn't really. "Now everyone grab your stuff and let's get going."

"Foxley Hill *ready*!" cheered the other team, doing their standing-in-a-circle handshake thing again.

"Ugh, that looks so stupid," said Wayne, glaring at them.

We all pulled on our rucksacks. Wayne and Chloe had both brought their own, but the rest of us were using the ancient and threadbare ones we'd borrowed from the school. I wouldn't have been surprised if these same rucksacks had been used in the original Wagstaffe Cup contest, decades ago.

Chloe's bag was bigger than everyone else's. She bent to pick it up, then thought better of it. "Hey, Wayne," she said, fluttering her mascara-coated eyelashes. "Would you do me a favour and carry my bag for me?"

"What? Yeah! Of course, no problem!" said Wayne, lunging for the bag. He grabbed a strap and swung it over his free shoulder, then almost toppled into the bushes. "Blimey, what's in it?" he asked.

"Just some make-up, shoes, a few changes of clothes, an iron… The necessities," said Chloe. "It's not too heavy, is it? I always thought you were really strong."

"Heavy? This?" Wayne squeaked, his face turning an uncomfortable shade of red. "Ha! I could carry this with my eyes shut."

"Well, yeah, because that wouldn't affect the

weight in the slightest, would it?" I said.

"Shut up, Beaky," Wayne wheezed. He forced a smile, despite the fact he was now leaning to one side and having to concentrate to walk in a straight line. "Now, let's get a move on."

"Yeah," I agreed. "Before your spine snaps in two."

And with that, we pushed on into the woods.

Twenty minutes later we stood in a clearing, trying to figure out which way up the map went. Mr Heft had led us to our drop-off spot, made us shut our eyes while he spun us in circles, then he'd disappeared into the woods, leaving us to fend for ourselves. To say it wasn't going well was a bit of an understatement.

"What do you mean, you can't read a map?" Wayne snapped. "I thought you were a survival expert?"

"Oh no, definitely not," I said.

"I sometimes get lost on the way to the shops. The closest I've ever come to wilderness survival is the time I fell in a bush and had to stay there for an hour until someone pulled me out."

"But ... what about the ferry?" Wayne asked.

"Oh, no, that was a complete lie," I admitted. "Sorry."

"Can you use a compass?"

"Only the ones you draw circles with," I said.

"Great!" said Wayne. "So now what do we do?"

"Here, let me see the map," said Evie. She spread it out on a fallen tree trunk and we all bent over to look at it. "What do we see?"

"A map," said Chloe.

"Yes, well spotted," said Evie. "But what do we see *on* the map?"

"Writing," Chloe said. "Little trees! A blue bit!"

"Our flag," said Theo, pointing to a little red flag-shaped sticker in the middle of a forest area.

"Exactly," said Evie.

"My stuff was right, too," Chloe pointed out.

"Yes, well done, Chloe," said Evie, shooting her an encouraging smile. "Really useful."

She shot me a sideways glance and half-rolled her eyes, then turned back to the map. I'd never really understood why Evie and Chloe were friends, since they had nothing in common and quite often didn't even seem to like each other very much. Still, they were inseparable. It was a bit like me and Theo,  I suppose. Only, you know, without the having nothing in common or not liking each other bit.

"So, our flag is here and this blue sticker is our campsite," said Evie.

"How do you know?" asked Wayne.

"Because it has the word 'campsite' written on it," she explained.

Wayne leaned in closer and squinted. "Oh. Right. Yeah." He straightened up. "So, what direction are they?"

Evie shrugged. "That, I don't know. I'm not sure

exactly where we are."

"In the foresty bit," said Chloe, gesturing vaguely to the wooded area of the map.

"I think she means where *specifically* are we?" said Theo. "As in, which direction do we need to go to find the flag?"

"Can't you ask the compass?" Chloe suggested.

"*Ask the compass*?" I spluttered. "It's not a Magic Eight Ball."

Chloe took the compass from me and studied it. "Can you work it?" Theo asked.

"It's broken," said Chloe, giving it a shake. "It just keeps pointing to the N."

"No," Evie began, then paused and sighed. "Yeah, you're right, it's broken."

"That's, like, *so* not fair," said Chloe. "Wherever we're going, we need to get there soon." She pointed down to her pristine white trainers. "All this grass and mud is doing my shoes no favours."

"Right, OK," Evie said. "So, does anyone have any idea how we can figure out where we are?"

There was some shuffling of feet, but no one replied.

"No, thought not," said Evie. "In that case, we're pretty much lost in the woods with no clue how to get to where we're going. Agreed?"

There was some muttering of agreement. "Yeah," said Wayne. "S'pose."

Evie shrugged. "Then I think we're going to have to radio Mr Heft for help."

"But then we'll lose the contest," Wayne protested.

"Better than losing our lives," Theo pointed out.

Wayne snorted. "Come on, it's not *that* bad. It's a forest, not the jungle!"

"Yeah, but it'll be getting dark soon," Theo said. "Hands up who fancies being out here in the dark without tents or anything."

Chloe's hand went up. She looked across at our faces. "Sorry, misunderstood the question," she said, then she quickly lowered her hand again.

"Right, that settles it, then," said Evie. "Wayne, get on the radio. Call Mr Heft and tell him we forfeit the contest."

"Wait," I said, as Wayne reached for the walkie-talkie on his belt. "Do we really want to do this? Do we really want to quit?"

"Yes," said Theo.

"Definitely," said Chloe.

"Not really," said Wayne.  "But what choice have we got? We don't know where to go."

I sighed. "Yeah. I know. It's just … we came so close. We're the first team to ever win a round against Foxley Hill. Imagine if we beat them!"

A hush fell across the clearing. "I mean, yeah, Wayne cheated so that we'd all be on the team, because he fancies Chloe and wants to beat me up," I said.

Chloe gasped. "Wayne? Is that true?"

"What? No!" Wayne blurted, his face turning red. That either meant he was embarrassed or close to exploding with rage. Probably both, I guessed. "I don't know what he's on about. I don't fancy you. Bleurgh! You're horrible!" he said, then he winced. "I mean, you're not *horrible* but… What I mean is…"

He grabbed for the walkie-talkie. "I'm calling Mr Heft. We should get out of here. Right now."

Wayne thumbed the button on the side of the radio. "Mr Heft. Come in, over."

He released the button. I'd expected to hear the hiss of static but the radio made no sound at all.

"Huh. That's weird," said Wayne, turning the power on and off. "It's not doing anything."

He turned the radio over. There was a soft click as he slid the battery compartment open.

"Uh-oh," I said, as we all stared down at the lifeless radio. "That's not good."

The walkie-talkie's battery compartment was empty.

CHAPTER 10

UPWARDLY MOBILE

"Right, let's not panic here, let's not panic," yelped Wayne, clearly panicking.

"Shouldn't that have, like, batteries in it or something?" asked Chloe.

"Yes!" said Evie. "Of course it should! But that's the problem – it doesn't."

"I bet the Foxley Hill kids nicked them," said Theo. "Probably in a way that involved acrobatics."

"Help!" bellowed Wayne, cupping his hands round his mouth. "Heeeeelp!"

We all listened. There was

no reply except the distant twitter of birds and something in the grass that might have been a frog.

"Where are the teachers?" Wayne babbled. "Heft said they'd be close by."

"Close enough for us to reach on the walkie-talkie, maybe," I guessed. "Not by shouting."

"We're going to die," Wayne announced. "We're all going to die!"

"So much for not panicking," said Evie.

I looked down at the map. The flag and the campsite were clearly marked. If only we could get a bird's eye view, like on the map, they'd be easy to spot.

I raised my head and looked up.

And up.

And up.

Tall trees towered around us, stretching almost to the sky. One tree in particular reached higher than the others.

"If someone climbed up there, they could figure out where we were," I announced.

Everyone turned to me, then followed my gaze to the treetops. Beside me, Wayne let out a little *cheep* of fear. He was scared of heights, as I'd discovered during the trip to Learning Land. I'd also discovered I wasn't all that keen on heights either, but I was nowhere near as terrified of them as Wayne.

"That's pretty high," said Theo.

"We should draw straws to see who's going to climb it," said Evie.

"What?" Wayne spluttered. "But we haven't even decided that's what we're doing yet."

Evie shrugged. "Can you think of a better plan?"

"Yes! I can think of twenty better plans!" said Wayne.

"Cool!" said Evie. "Name one."

Wayne hesitated. He cupped his hands round his mouth. "Heeeeelp!" he cried.

"Yeah, thought not," said Evie, bending down and grabbing some long straw-like blades of grass. "Right, five of us, five straws," she said, holding her hand out. Five pieces of grass poked from the top of her clenched fist. "Four are the same length, one's shorter. Whoever gets the short straw climbs the tree. Who wants to go first?"

Chloe elbowed past me and Theo. "I'm first!" she said. She stared intently at Evie's hand for a while, as if she was trying to develop X-ray vision using willpower alone. Then, with a quick *yank* she pulled out a straw. "Is this … is this the short one?" she asked.

"No," said Evie. "It's not."

Chloe thrust both hands in the air and let out a loud *whoop* of delight. "In your faces, suckers!" she yelled, then she composed herself. "By which I mean, OMG, that's a relief."

"Theo?" said Evie.

144

After flexing his fingers a few times, Theo reached for one of the blades of grass. Everyone held their breath.

Theo changed his mind and reached for a different blade of grass instead.

Everyone held their breath.

"No, not that one," Theo muttered, changing his mind again.

"Just hurry up!" Wayne barked. Theo plucked one of the blades free. It was the same length as Chloe's. He grinned, happily. Wayne groaned.

"It's going to be me. I just know it."

"It might not be," I said, reaching for one of the straws. I pulled it free. It was full-length. "No, you're right, it's going to be you," I said.

"Might not," said Evie. There were just two blades of grass left now. She held her clenched fist out to Wayne. "Might be me. Let's find out."

Wayne stared at the offered straws, his eyes bulging, his face fixed in an expression of utter terror.

"I … I don't know which one to pick."

"Just pick one," I said. "Any one."

"But I might pick the wrong one!"

"OMG, it's only a tree," said Chloe.

Wayne tried to smile but his mouth was dead set against the idea. Slowly he reached out a hand. His fingertips tightened round the end of one of the straws. He closed his eyes, took a deep breath, then pulled.

"It's the short one!" I announced. Wayne made a sound like an airbed springing a leak and stumbled back, staring in horrified disbelief at the half-sized blade of grass in his hand.

"No, but … I didn't mean to pick that one. I meant to pick the other one," he said. "Put it back in and we'll do it again."

"No chance," said Evie. "You lost, Wayne. Up the tree you go."

Shaking his head, Wayne leaned back and looked up at the tree.

146

"Wow," I said quietly. "It's proper high, isn't it?"

"Shut up, Beaky!" Wayne hissed. "This is your fault!"

"What? How is it my fault?"

"Because you're the one who suggested someone should climb up!"

"Oh. Yeah," I said. "You're right, it is my fault." I flashed him a smile. "Sorry."

To my surprise, Wayne didn't snarl or growl or try to punch me into next week. Instead he just looked … sad or something. The hard-man act he always put on had fallen away, revealing a scared kid underneath. He turned away so Chloe wouldn't notice.

"You really don't like heights, do you?" I whispered.

"What? Shut up," he said, the act returning for just a moment. Then he shook his head. "No."

I glanced up at the tree again. It really was ridiculously high. The thought of Wayne having to

147

climb it should have made me happy and yet...
He'd clapped for me at the debate. He'd been the
first person to applaud, even though – and I really
can't stress this enough – he hated my guts.

After everything he'd put me through over the
years, he deserved to be sent up that tree and he
deserved the total humiliation of failing to climb it.

And yet...

It was like with Mrs Munn's Christmas present,
I suppose – sometimes, you have to say and do
things you don't really want to because it's the
right thing to do. Even if that means letting Wayne
Lawson off the hook.

I sighed. "Fine," I muttered, then I raised my
voice. "I'll do it."

Wayne's head snapped round.
"What?"

"I'll do it. I'll climb the tree."

Theo frowned. "Why?" he
asked.

I knew I had to choose my

148

next words carefully. If I just blurted out the first thing my truth-telling brain came up with, Wayne would think I was trying to humiliate him in front of Chloe and would probably beat me up, then force me to climb the tree anyway. If I was careful about what I said, I might at least avoid the part where I got a beating.

"Because being part of a team is all about using the right people for the right job," I said. "I'm better at climbing than Wayne, so it makes sense for me to go up there."

Wayne's eyes widened and his jaw dropped.

"Is that OK with you, Wayne?" I asked.

Wayne nodded, slowly at first then quickly growing more enthusiastic. "Uh, yes. I mean, if you want, yeah. I don't mind, really."

"Oh, well, if you don't mind…" I began, but a yelp from Wayne cut me off.

"No! I mean, yeah, maybe you should go.

It makes more sense. Teamwork and all that."

"Yeah, teamwork and all that," I agreed, shrugging off my rucksack and taking hold of the first few branches. "Also, you looked like you were about to wet yourself, so there's that, too."

"Be careful, Beaky," said Evie.

"Yeah, don't fall and break your legs or anything," added Theo.

"Thanks for that," I said. "I'll try not to."

And then, with a final look up at the treetops towering overhead, I began to climb.

CHAPTER 11

UP A TREE

The first ... ooh ... seventy-five per cent or so of the plan went perfectly. Climbing the tree was pretty easy because of the way its branches were positioned and I made it to the top after just a few minutes.

From up there I could see the whole world. At least, that was how it felt. I could spot both our flag and Foxley Hill's. They were on poles in clearings – ours a violent shade of purple, theirs a sort of faded orange.

As well as the flags, I could also see both campsites and the obstacle course we'd have to tackle in the morning. None of it was all that far away.

I shouted down directions to Theo, who scribbled them on the map. "OK, got it!" he called, his voice distant and faint. And that was when I discovered the problem.

"Ooh, it's high," I croaked, looking down at the ground. It seemed a ridiculous distance away. Theo and the others were barely bigger than bugs, and what had been a pretty easy climb up now looked like an impossible climb down.

"Slight problem," I announced. "I'm completely stuck."

"*Find meaty luck?*" Theo shouted. "What does that mean?"

I raised my voice. "No! I said I'm completely stuck. I can't get down!"

There was some murmuring I couldn't make out as they discussed this. The tree creaked as the wind nudged it back and forth. I wrapped both arms round the trunk and held on for dear life.

"Have you tried?" Theo shouted.

"Can't. Completely paralysed by fear," I shouted back. "I think … I think I'll just live here now."

"Could you jump and use your jacket as a parachute?" Chloe shouted.

"Yes," I replied. "But I'd die."

"Oh," said Chloe, disappointed. "You sure?"

"Pretty sure," I said. "Also, I left my jacket down there."

More murmuring. A large, boggle-eyed bird landed on a branch just a metre or so away from me. It tilted its head, sizing me up.

"All right?" I said. "Er… Come here often?"

The bird hopped closer. I'm not really sure what sort of bird it was but its beak was pretty large and there was an evil glint in its dark eyes that suggested it was trying to figure out how to get me back to its nest for dinner.

To eat me for dinner, I mean, not as a guest.

"Shoo," I said, as it took another hop towards me. My arms and legs were fully occupied with hugging the tree, so I blew at the bird, trying to scare it away. It didn't work. The bird let out a low *rrrawrk* sound, then scraped at the branch with its long, curved claws.

"Good birdie. Nice birdie," I whispered.

"All right, Beaky?" said Evie, suddenly appearing below me. I screamed and almost lost my grip as she scrabbled up the last few branches. The sudden flurry of movement scared off the bird and with a final evil glare it took to the air.

"How did you get up here so fast?" I gasped.

"I climbed," said Evie. "It's pretty easy."

"Right, well, whatever you do, don't look down," I told her.

Evie looked down. "It is pretty high, isn't it?" she said. "We might need to give each other a hand to get to the bottom."

I nodded nervously. The thought of climbing down was still terrifying but now that I had company, I wasn't quite so frozen by fear. Maybe I wouldn't have to live in a tree for the rest of my life, after all.

"It was pretty cool what you did," said Evie.

"What? Getting stuck up a tree?"

"No, climbing the tree in the first place," she said. "Personally, I'd have let Wayne do it and laughed when he got stuck at the second branch but ... it was pretty cool that you didn't."

"Oh," I said. "Thanks."

Evie looked out across the trees. "Wow, you can see for miles up here." She frowned. "Hey, look.

Foxley Hill are taking both flags."

I followed her gaze and, sure enough, Foxley Hill had split up into two groups. One group was in the clearing beside their own flag, while two of the pupils – we were too far away to see which – were untying our flag!

"The dirty cheats!" I yelped. "If we don't have our flag when we get over the finish line tomorrow, we can't win."

Evie smiled at me. "Then we'll just have to get it back, won't we?" she said. "But first, we should probably try to get down."

I swallowed and nodded.

"Not that I'm in a rush," Evie said. "It's nice up here – the view and everything. We could stay a bit longer, if you like."

"I'm about four minutes away from wetting myself," I said. "Or possibly worse."

Evie considered this for a moment. "Yeah. Let's climb down," she said.

With Evie leading the way and me whimpering and yelping every twenty seconds or so, we clambered back down to the ground. As soon as my feet hit the forest floor, I fell over and spent the next two minutes hugging the mud.

Then, once that was done, I jumped to my feet and went tearing into the bushes, frantically tugging at the button of my trousers.

"It's OK!" I announced. "It's just a number one."

"Ew. We don't want to know," Chloe said. She started singing to drown out any noises I made and when I returned to the clearing I found her with her fingers jammed in her ears.

"Evie says Foxley Hill have nicked our flag!" Wayne snapped. "Is that true?"

"Yeah," I said.

Wayne cracked his knuckles. A grin crept across his face. "Right, then we're going to get it back."

"How?" I asked.

"Like you said, we've all got our own skills. You're good at climbing trees," Wayne said.

"Well, good-*ish*," said Chloe. "He did get stuck."

"Good point, well made, Chloe," said Wayne, switching his smile from "wicked grin" to "simpering idiot". It only took him a second to change it back again. "You're good-ish at climbing trees and I'm good at getting flags back."

"Are you?" I said. "Really? Have you ever got a flag back before?"

Wayne frowned. "What?"

"I mean ... it seems quite an unusual thing to have had much experience in," I said.

"I've never even had a flag before, never mind had to get it back off someone."

"Shut up," Wayne growled. "I meant I'm good at teaching people a lesson when they try to cross me. And Foxley Hill just crossed us bad."

"We should come up with a plan," said Theo. "To get it back."

"Yeah, we should do that," I said. As the others started forming a huddle, I leaned closer to Theo. "There's just one problem," I said. "If anyone from Foxley Hill asks me what the plan is, I'll tell them. I won't be able to help it."

Theo nodded slowly. "Yeah, good point," he said. "I didn't think of that. Leave it with me."

Then, just before we went to join the others in their plan-forming huddle, Theo shot me a smirk. "Oh, and before I forget," he whispered, then he began to sing quietly: "Beaky and Evie sitting in a tree..."

CHAPTER 12

THE RAID

That night, after we'd eventually found our camp, got our campfire started, eaten the food the school canteen had supplied (lovingly prepared by Miss Gavistock, I hoped) and Mr Heft had come to check on us to make sure we were all still alive, we hunkered down in our tents and grabbed a few hours' sleep before making our move.

At least, I tried to sleep, but as I had to share a tent with Wayne and Theo, Wayne's constant snoring and Theo's twice-a-minute farting made it pretty much impossible. Even without them,

PPAAARRRP

ZZZZZZZ

PARP

PARP

getting to sleep would have been difficult. The tents were even more ancient than the rucksacks and the roof lining kept sagging against my head every few minutes.

Just after 3 a.m., the alarm on Wayne's watch went off and it was time to put the plan into action.

Chloe opened up her immense rucksack, revealing about two hundred little boxes and tubs, all containing different make-up. She set to work plastering Theo and me with layers of brown and green eye shadow. By the time she was finished, our faces looked practically invisible against the trees. Of course, the fact the forest was in near-total darkness helped, too.

"Nice camouflage," said Wayne. "Great work, Chloe. You're really talented."

"Yes," said Chloe, leaning back to admire her handiwork. "I am, aren't I?"

Chloe turned to Wayne and Evie. "OK, now..." she began but I yelped and clamped my hands over my ears so I couldn't hear what she said next.

I knew the first part of the plan – get make-up on and follow Theo into the woods – but because I wouldn't be able to keep the rest of it secret, I'd made sure Theo didn't tell me any more. The last thing I wanted was to accidentally shout out the whole plan as we were sneaking into camp.

"We'll get going," said Theo, taking me by the arm. It was well past four o'clock by now and if we didn't make our move soon, the sun would be starting to rise.

"Good luck, Beaky," said Evie.

Theo stared at her expectantly.

"Uh, both of you, I mean," she said. She blushed slightly, then quickly turned away. Theo grinned at me and waggled his eyebrows, then we flicked on our head torches and set off into the dark woods.

Mr Heft had given us a "refresher course" on using the map and compass after Theo had pointed out that I'd had neither of those things when I'd survived in the wilderness following the make-believe ferry incident.

I'd kept well out of the teacher's way, in case I'd had the urge to spill the beans about the stolen flag. We could have told him, of course – that would have been the sensible thing to do – but Wayne was determined we were going to get it back ourselves and teach the Foxley Hill mob a lesson in the process.

Fifteen minutes of clambering through the woods later, we spotted the flickering glow of the Foxley Hill campfire and quickly switched off our torches. The camp was quiet, as you might expect given it was still the middle of the night, and there was no sign of our flag anywhere.

"OK, now what?" I whispered.

Theo patted me on the back. "Now, I'm going back to the camp and you're going to stay here."

 "What?" I said. "Why? Wait, don't tell me!"

163

"It's OK, I wasn't going to," Theo said, backing off into the woods. "Just stay here and pretend to be a bush or a tree or something. That's what the camouflage is for. Pretend you're not here."

"Pretend I'm…? But Theo, that's like lying! How can I…?"

There was no point continuing. Theo had disappeared into the forest, leaving me all alone.

I looked back at the Foxley Hill camp. "Pretend to be a bush or a tree or something," I said to myself.

My left leg took a jerky step towards the camp. *Oh no.*

"Pretend I'm not here."

My right leg followed the left, then the left one pulled ahead again. Like a puppet, I began lurching faster and faster towards the Foxley Hill camp.

"I'm not a bush!" I shouted, my voice echoing through the woods as the truth escaped from my lips. "I'm not a bush or a tree. I'm definitely here!"

I stumbled out of the woods just as the zips on the Foxley Hill tents were yanked down. Malcolm dived through the door of one, kicking free of his sleeping bag. Jessica pulled off a perfect forwards roll as she emerged from the other tent, then leaped up into a fighting stance,  ready for danger.

"What do you want?" Malcolm demanded. His face looked angry in the flickering glow of the campfire.

"Hello! I've come to steal the flag back," I announced. "That's why I'm wearing make-up. I don't usually wear make-up but – between you and me – it's actually quite fun. I'm supposed to be a tree."

"A tree?" Malcolm frowned.

"Or a bush. One of those."

The rest of the Foxley Hill team charged out of their tents and gathered round me. Through a gap in the door flap of the boys' tent, the firelight picked out a corner of purple material – our flag!

"Who's with you?" asked Malcolm. "There's no way you came alone."

I shook my head. "No, I came with my mate, Theo, but he ran off into the woods somewhere and left me to spy on you."

Felicity and a couple of the others turned to look into the woods but saw no sign of movement anywhere.

"So where are the others now?" said Malcolm.

I shrugged. "I don't know."

"What do you mean, *you don't know*?" Malcolm growled, towering over me. He really was ridiculously tall for his age.

"If you're trying to scare me, it's totally working," I squeaked.

"Then tell me where everyone is!"

"I can't. I don't know," I said. "They were at our camp when me and Theo left but I don't know if they're still there."

Malcolm grabbed me by the front of my jacket. The glow of the firelight flickered across his face, making him look even scarier than he actually was. "So what's your plan, then?"

"I don't know," I said. "All they told me was the bit about getting my face painted and going into the woods with Theo. See, I have this … condition, which means I can't lie."

The Foxley Hill pupils all glanced at each other in confusion. "D'you expect us to believe that?" asked Felicity.

"It's true!" I babbled. "If I knew the plan, I'd already have spilled it to you. That's why I made sure they didn't tell me it," I said. I couldn't fight the grin that spread like a rash across my face. "I have literally no idea what's going to happen next," I said.

With a *hiss*, the fire went out and the camp was plunged into darkness.

I giggled. "But I bet it's going to be exciting."

CHAPTER 13

MONSTERS ATTACK!

Three floating heads emerged from the trees, their faces ghostly white and shining in the darkness. They bobbed towards us, their eyes in shadow and something that looked like blood dripping from their mouths.

"Who's that?" whispered one of the Foxley Hill boys who wasn't Malcolm. I'm sure he had a name but right then I was too shocked to remember it.

"It's them, you idiot!" said Malcolm,

but there was a note of something in his voice that suggested he wasn't completely convinced.

"How can it be them?" yelped Felicity. "They're floating heads!"

She screamed and jumped into the air. "My leg! Something touched my leg!"

Everyone, including me, looked down but it was impossible to see anything through the darkness.

"All right, calm down," Malcolm snapped. "It's just them trying to freak us out."

"Where did they go?" asked the other not-Malcolm. "The faces? Where did they go?"

We all looked round. Sure enough, the floating heads had vanished! Everyone turned and searched the woods for any sign of movement. It was far too dark to see more than a few centimetres beyond our own noses, though and as the blackness pushed in on us, I could practically hear everyone's hearts pounding.

Wayne and the others had really outdone themselves. Even *I* was starting to get a bit scared.

"I don't like this," said Felicity. "Show yourselves!"

There was a soft *click* behind her. A vision of pure terror appeared, floating a full two-and-a-half metres in the air. A glowing white face with dark eyes and a blood-ringed mouth peered down at us.

"Boo!" it said, and then it vanished.

That did it. Everyone but me and Malcolm shot off in different directions, stumbling blindly through the dark.

"Don't let them get me!"

"It's a monster!"

"H-help!"

"Come back here, you cowards!" Malcolm roared. "It's them. They're playing a trick on us. There's no such thing as..."

The face appeared again, this time nearer ground level. "Hello, Malcolm," said Wayne, but before Malcolm could react, his sleeping bag was yanked down over his head. Off-balance, he toppled backwards and landed on the ground. Theo and Evie quickly zipped the sleeping bag round his feet as he thrashed about like an angry worm in an effort to get free.

Up close, I could see the torch tucked into the neck of Wayne's jacket. It cast a spooky glow across his white-painted face. "Good, huh?" he said. "Told you I'm an expert at getting flags back."

"You were huge a minute ago," I said. "How did you do that?"

Theo's torch clicked on, lighting up his face. "He was on my shoulders," he said, grinning.

There was another *click* and Evie's face lit up so close to me I let out a little squeal of fright. "Sorry," she said, smirking. "Didn't mean to scare you."

"I've got it!" said Chloe, emerging from the boys' tent and passing the flag to Wayne.

"Great work, Chloe! That was really helpful," Wayne said. He tried to give her a celebratory hug but she ducked past him and set off towards the trees.

"Come on, let's get back to camp!" she said. "I forgot to pack away the make-up and I'm scared the squirrels might get it."

As the others headed back to camp, I clicked on my head torch and aimed it down at Malcolm. He was still flopping about in his sleeping bag, desperately trying to break free.

"D'you know, I really enjoyed this," I said, completely truthfully. "Let's do it again some time!"

After a few wrong turns, we made it back to camp just as the sun was coming up. We collapsed on to the grass, exhausted but happy. We'd done it! We'd got our flag back! Now we could get a couple of hours' rest before...

HOOOOOOOOONK!

"What's that noise?" asked Theo, looking around.

"A massive goose?" I guessed.

"It's the alarm," Evie realized. "It means we're supposed to race to the obstacle course!"

"What, *now*?" Chloe groaned. "But look at the state of my hair. OMG, how am I supposed to face people like this? Proper people who matter, I mean, not you lot. No offence."

"Loads taken," I said, clambering to my feet. My legs had been aching ever since the climb up and down the tree. All the rest of me ached, too, now that I thought about it. "I really want to have a lie down," I said. "And maybe some light medical assistance. But I'm not going to."

Wayne was still on the ground, catching his breath. Despite everything that had ever happened between us, I held a hand out to him. "Because we've got a contest to win."

We scrambled into the assault course clearing in time to see the Foxley Hill pupils all darting across

173

the first obstacle – a narrow balance beam over a large muddy puddle.

Their PE teacher, Mr Mann, jogged along beside them, his voice snapping like a whip. "Faster. Move. Go. Now."

Meanwhile our PE teacher, Mrs Moir, was trying with very little success to get up from her camping chair. "On you go," she urged, waving us on. "I'll be right behind you. Be careful!"

Evie leaped on to the balance beam and raced across it without any problems. Chloe went next, wobbling unsteadily. Her trainers didn't look very new any more, thanks to the layer of mud covering them.

Theo, Wayne and I all followed and by the time I jumped down, Evie was throwing herself at the rope swing and swooping across the water obstacle like Tarzan.

"Move. Move. Faster. Swing." Mr Mann was roaring at the Foxley Hill kids, driving them on.

Evie threw back the rope and Chloe caught it.

174

She stared down at the puddle. "What if I fall in?"

"You won't," Wayne soothed.

"I might!" Chloe argued.

"Let's find out," I said, stepping forwards and giving her a shove. She screamed as she went soaring over the water, then Evie caught her on the other side.

"We're catching them," said Wayne, grabbing the rope. "Come on, hurry up, we can do this!"

He swung across. Theo went next, then me. I let go of the rope swing and turned to find Wayne at the foot of the next obstacle, his face white with fear.

It was a net.

A very high net.

And Chloe and Evie were already halfway to the top.

Theo hurled himself after them and scrambled up. The Foxley Hill team were already up and over and running towards the final obstacle. "Come on, Wayne, you can do it," I said.

Wayne shook his head. His mouth moved but no sound came out. His face was pale, and not just because of the ghost make-up still plastered on his face.

Taking my life in my hands, I grabbed him by his collar, like he'd done to me so many times before. "Move!" I barked, dragging him towards the net.

At first, he tried to push back but then he grabbed the net with both hands. The only way we could win is if he got over that thing and he knew it.

"Now climb, Wayne!" I told him. "Climb like the wind! Only, you know, with arms and legs and stuff."

"I … I can't."

"Just do what I do. Watch!" I said.

I put a foot on the net and immediately slipped right through. My groin met the rope at high speed, then I fell backwards, dangling from the net.

"OK," I wheezed. "Not *exactly* like that."

With help from Wayne, I pulled myself free. Theo and Evie dropped down on to the other side of the net. "Hurry up," Evie said. "Come on!"

"Help!"

We all looked up to see Chloe flapping around at the top of the net. Her foot had slipped through just like mine and she was hanging by one leg, several metres above the ground.

Evie moved to climb back up but I shook my head. "No, you keep going. I'll get her," I said. I was about to climb when I felt Wayne's hand on my shoulder.

"No," he said. "*I'll* get her."

Wayne began to climb. For a moment, it was like I was seeing him clamber up in dramatic slow-motion, but then I realized that he actually was moving at that speed. I hurried past him, looped over the top, and flashed the upside-down Chloe a smile. "Help's on the way!" I told her, then I dropped down and set off after Theo and Evie.

The final obstacle was made up of six tractor tyres, all hanging from ropes and positioned at different heights. Theo and Evie were squeezing themselves through the tyres but the Foxley Hill team had almost finished now. Malcolm was already racing towards the finish line, with Felicity not far behind.

I glanced back at the net. Wayne was at the top, sitting astride the wooden rail. He pulled Chloe back up and together they unhooked her leg.

"You saved me!" she gasped. "Wayne, you saved me!"

Wayne beamed from ear to ear. "I did it! I climbed the net!"

He threw his arms in the air. "I'm unstoppable!" he cried, before he immediately fell off and landed with a *splut* in the mud.

It took us just a couple of minutes to get everyone through the tyres but by then it was too late. The finish line was about a third of a kilometre up ahead and a cheer went up as one of the non-Malcolms crossed it.

"Well, that's it, then," I said.

It was over.

Foxley Hill had won.

"Might as well just walk it now," said Wayne.

"No way! Are you kidding?" said Chloe. We all turned to look at her and she blushed, just a little, beneath her ghostly-white make-up. We hadn't had a chance to wash the stuff off before the alarm sounded. "I mean ... we've come this far, right? We might as well finish properly."

We all considered this for a moment.

"Sounds good to me," said Theo.

"I'm in," Evie said.

"I'll give it a go but I'm really tired and I might be sick," I said.

"Yeah, let's do it," said Wayne. We all began to move but he stopped us. "Wait!" he said, looking a little embarrassed. He held his hand out in front of him, palm down.

It took me a second to figure out what he was doing, then I stepped in and put my hand on top of his. "This is probably the worst team I've ever been in for anything," I said. "But I'm glad I'm part of it."

"Shut up, you big girl," Wayne said, but the way he grinned told me he didn't mean it. Probably.

Evie put her hand on top of mine, then Theo and Chloe joined in. "Everyone ready?" said Theo.

"Ready," we all said.

"Hello, everyone!" panted Mrs Moir, staggering

up to join us just as we all broke into a run. "Oh! Very good. Off you go. Right behind you," she wheezed.

We ran together to the finish line, linking arms just before we crossed it. A half-hearted cheer went up from a small group of supporters who had turned up to watch. Mr Lawson was there, of course, with my mum and dad standing beside him. Even Jodie had come to see us finish, but she had been given Destructo to look after and was standing well back from everyone else in case he tried to eat them.

Chloe and Theo's parents were there, too. Evie's mum stood on the opposite side of Mr Lawson to my mum and dad. Mrs Green and Mum swapped dirty looks behind the head teacher's back, as they each tried to clap louder than the other.

"Well done, team!" said Mum.

"Yes, congratulations," said Mrs Green. "On behalf of—"

"*Theparentteacherassociation*," Mum quickly blurted over her, all in one breath.

There were only a couple of Foxley Hill parents there, along with the elf-like Miss Garden and the terrifying Mr Mann. They'd won the contest every year since it started, so it probably wasn't even a big deal to them any more, I guessed.

Mr Heft smiled and gave us a thumbs up. "Great work, guys," he said. At first, I assumed he was being sarcastic but  on closer inspection I realized he actually meant it.

"Yes, good effort, team," said Mr Lawson, applauding politely. "It was a close-run thing."

"Sorry, Dad," said Wayne, hanging his head. "I know how much you wanted us to win. We let you down."

Mr Lawson's eyes went wide. "What? Let me

down? No one let me down!" he said. "You're the first team in our school's history to win a single round against Foxley Hill. You came within less than a minute of winning the whole thing!" He looked across us all and smiled. "I honestly could not be prouder," he said. "Although ... why is everyone wearing make-up?"

"Long story," said Theo, butting in before I could explain everything.

"Can we get on with it, *sir*?" said Malcolm, and I felt Wayne tense beside me. "We'd like our prizes now."

Mr Lawson smiled sadly. "Yes. Of course," he said. He reached into a cardboard box and pulled out a shiny silver trophy. There were lots of inscriptions on the front of it. They all said "Foxley Hill School" then a date beneath.

After gazing at it longingly for a moment, Mr Lawson held up the trophy. "It gives me great pleasure to present the Winston and Watson Wagstaffe Cup of Competitive Chummery to this year's winners, Foxley Hill."

Malcolm took the trophy eagerly and sneered as he waved it at us. "Better luck next time," he cackled.

"And now for the medals," said Mr Lawson, reaching into the box again and fishing out five gold medals.

The audience all clapped as one by one Mr Lawson placed the medals over the Foxley Hill pupils' heads. "Malcolm. Felicity," he said, nodding at them sadly as he presented each one. "Jessica. Christopher."

He stopped then, the final medal clutched in his hands. He looked around. "Where's Edgar?"

Malcolm frowned and looked along the line. "What? He's… Where is he?"

"Coo-ee!" called Mrs Moir. She shuffled towards the finish line, leading a wide-eyed Edgar by the arm. "Just found him wandering in the woods," she said. "Mumbling something about floating heads."

Beside me, Mr Lawson and Wayne both gasped at the same time. "Hang on!" said Mr Lawson.

"The whole Foxley Hill team didn't cross the finish line!" blurted Wayne.

"Yes!" I said, punching my fist in the air. I lowered it again. "What does that mean?"

"As per the rules of the contest, in order for a

team to be deemed as having completed the final assault course challenge, all members of said team must cross the finish line," Mr Lawson babbled.

"Yes!" I said, punching my fist in the air again. And again, I lowered it. "What does that mean?"

"It means we won, dummy!" Evie laughed. She threw her arms round me and I felt Theo do the same. Chloe and Wayne piled on next and we all bounced up and down, cheering and whooping with delight.

"I'm about to have a panic attack!" I announced, as they squashed in on me. One by one they pulled away, until only Evie remained. Blushing, she untangled herself and we both turned to see Mr Lawson taking the medals and trophy back from the Foxley Hill team.

"It gives me *enormous* pleasure to declare that the winner of this year's inter-schools contest is Nutley Grange!" said Mr Lawson, placing the medals over our heads.

"Watch the hair," Chloe muttered, and even Mr Lawson couldn't help but laugh. I looked across at Mum and Dad. They were both beaming from ear to ear. Behind them, Jodie gave me a thumbs up, then almost had her arm yanked out of the socket as Destructo set off after a squirrel.

After a few well-earned minutes rubbing our victory in Foxley Hill's faces, Mr Heft gave us our phones back. Chloe grabbed hers eagerly and hugged it like a long-lost relative.  "Oh, I've missed you," she said, half sobbing.

"I'm sure you'll want to take 'selfies' of each other with your medals," said Mr Lawson, smiling.

"You can't take selfies of another person," I pointed out. "Those are called 'photographs'."

"Right, yes," said Mr Lawson.

"You tried to be young and trendy there and it backfired quite badly, sir," I pointed out.

Mr Lawson grimaced. "Yes. Quite," he said, then he about-turned and marched off to talk to the assembled teachers and parents.

Wayne, Chloe, Evie, Theo and me all stood in a circle, admiring our medals. "Wayne, I still don't know why you arranged for us all to be on the same team but it paid off," I said.

Wayne looked at me strangely. "What?"

"You rigged the choices," I said. "You planted our names."

Wayne shook his head. "No, I didn't."

"Yes, you did," I insisted. "You must have."

"No," said Wayne, looking genuinely confused. "I did think it was pretty weird but it wasn't me."

"What? Seriously?" I said. It couldn't just have been coincidence. "Then who was it?"

My phone buzzed in my hand. I looked down to find the subject line of an email staring up at me.

"RE: Madame Shirley."

Madame Shirley? Before I could read it, Dad appeared beside us. He had his guitar in his hands and winked at me as he strummed a few chords.

"Oh no," I groaned.

"I've taken the liberty of writing a little victory song," he said. He cleared his throat, winked at me again, then began to play.

"They're amazing,

They're stupendous,

Whenever there's a contest they'll be—"

He stopped with a *twang* and let the guitar swing down on the strap. "Argh! That's still *Danger Mouse*," he said, then he shrugged and smiled. "Still, it's the thought that counts, right?"

He turned and walked back to Mum. As I tapped my phone's screen to read the email Evie appeared beside me. "Hey, Beaky," she said, shuffling awkwardly from side to side. "I just wanted to say … it was cool to hang out."

And then, to my amazement/horror/delight, she leaned in and kissed me on the cheek.

I opened my mouth to say something but for the first time ever, nothing came out. No lies. No truth. No nothing.

"I'll see you at school," Evie said, then she turned and hurried to join her mum.

"See?" said Theo. "Told you."

I watched Mrs Green and Mum shoot daggers at each other again, then Evie gave me a little wave. I waved back and smiled.

"Theo, I have the feeling my life is about to become even more complicated," I whispered, then I stared down at the email and realized just how right I was.

There were four words. Four words that made the whole forest spin around me. Four words that might just change my life forever.

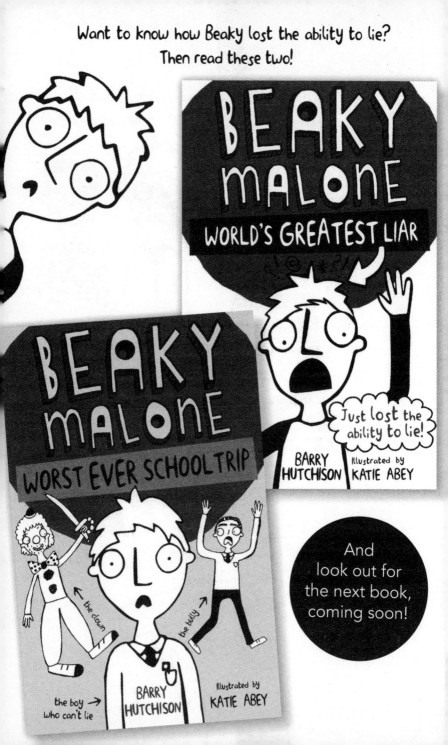